
UNSTOPPABLE

UNSTOPPABLE

THE NATURE OF GRACE
BOOK 3

SHELLI R. JOHANNES

*To all the brave people who work to
protect and save animals everyday.*

$$\text{\large\textbf{PROLOGUE}}$$

There is no place like the Everglades in the world.

The Everglades is a far cry from the Smoky Mountains.

For every tree in the mountains, there's an alligator in the swamps.

As I slog through the hip-deep water, my heartbeat sloshes in my ears. I stay on high alert, sifting through the creepy sounds. The chirp of a tree frog, the hammering of the woodpecker, and the splash of a turtle as he slides into the murky water.

Even though I've been in the Glades for a month, every sound still sends my heart skittering. My mind only thinks one thing...*alligators.*

I use my walking stick to poke at a raft of vegetation floating off to one side. Little bugs and beetles scoot out from underneath and skim across the surface, making a quick escape. I take another step and pull my body through the lukewarm water. I jerk my head to the right and eye a few ripples until they disappear. This place messes with my head. The swamp water drowns any logic as fear bobs along the surface. The creepy critters and dynamic terrain are hard enough to deal with, but the loneliness is far worse.

How long has it been? A day? Two? I've lost count.

If I could find the others, I'd have a much better chance of surviving this mess. But right now, I don't have a fair shot. Being alone out here, I know the odds are stacked against me.

I bite my bottom lip to keep from crying and slip through the slime and sludge. My knees tremble with every uncertain step I take toward the far embankment. My feet trudge through the heavy silt blanketing the swampy floor. Only a few more yards and I'll finally be on dry land. I need to get out of this water, or I'll surely get a nasty case of trench foot.

A low, grumbling noise drowns out the swamp's melody. I stop in mid-stride and grip my stick with both hands, knuckles white. The way alligators growl mimics a really pissed off lion. It's one of the scariest—most horrifying—sounds I've ever heard. Especially when it's nearing dusk and I'm standing in dark water that is chest deep.

With arms raised in a striking position, I scan the pitch-black water, expecting a huge gator to snatch me from underneath and drag me down into the murky abyss.

Dylan's gator tips scroll through my head.

1. *Don't get dragged into the water.*
2. *Avoid the death roll.*
3. *Always try to fight on land.*

Or not at all, if you ask me.

After watching Rex's nephew, Dylan, perform his suicidal stunts at Alligator Land, I now know there are only two ways to defeat an alligator if forced into hand-to-hand combat.

1. Punch it on top of the head until it lets go.
2. Jam your fist so far down its throat that it drowns.

To me, number one doesn't sound very promising, considering an alligator's skin is hard and protected with small, rigid bones. And the second option is just stupid and plain impossible.

I hold my breath, listening for another sound to crack the silence.

After a few seconds, I wade forward one step at a time, knowing each one could be my last. And I wouldn't see any attack until it was too late. I can't help but be gripped by total terror, not knowing what's hiding under the water or in the shadows. Even though I want to rush—get the hell out of this swamp—I fight against my natural flight instincts and focus on keeping my pace slow and even.

Finally, after three and a half heart attacks, the water gets shallower until I reach the thin shore. I jam my stick into the soft, silty mud and grab a low hanging vine for support. Slowly, I drag my body out of the water. My legs ache, weighted down by waterlogged pants and soaking wet shoes.

I yank and pull and push until I'm free. I scramble onto the shore and quickly scoot away from the water's edge. When no scaly monster follows, I lean against a dead cypress tree to catch my breath.

Walking through those swamps was one of the scariest moments of my life.

Not counting all those with Al in them.

Sometimes the not knowing—combined with my overactive imagination—is worse than an actual event. Now, even though I'm temporarily safe, I can't relax until I escape these swamps. I remain as alert as I can, though my brain is muddled. I haven't eaten much, so the dehydration and hunger are starting to wear me down, making me weak.

Making me vulnerable.

I scan the still horizon of the water's glassy surface, searching for any sign of a predator. Bubbles. Ripples. Glowing eyes.

In the Everglades, I've learned one thing...you are never truly safe.

Whether you're on dry land or stuck in the swamps.

My body goes limp as exhaustion tries to settle in for the night. I jolt upright and shake my head, trying to stay awake. Alert. No matter how much I want to sleep or lie down for just a second, I can't risk it. Especially not here.

If I do, I may never get out alive. I may never see Mo again.

I stand and fight my way up the steep ,slippery hill. Every few minutes, I can't help but scan the water behind me for any signs of a last minute attack.

Out here, you can never let your guard down.

Animals wait for it.

Behind me, a few gunshots sound off in the distance. I dive into the thick underbrush to hide.

This sick game of cat and mouse has gone on long enough.

No matter how far away these men are, it's still too close for comfort. Another surge of adrenaline releases into my veins. Surprised I have any left at this point.

Lying on my stomach, I breathe evenly and check my compass. No choice but to take the long way out if I want to avoid any more nasty confrontations. I can't have another death on my hands. Even though the swamp grows darker and more dangerous by the minute, I never prefer running into crazies.

I'd rather fight an alligator face-to-face than get gunned down from a distance.

Just as I make a plan and get the nerve to head out, something rustles in the bushes on the other side of the path.

I grab my stick and plant both feet, ready for anything. Or anyone. No matter what comes at me, I can't hesitate. If I do, it could be the difference between deaths.

It's either them or me.

If given a chance, I guess it's better to kill than be killed. Not a motto I choose to live by, but one that's been forced on me over the last year. Especially in the last day.

A shadow slides through the thick vegetation.

I keep one hand on the big stick and slowly reach into my boot with the other—careful not to move too much. I slide out the large knife Tommy gave me last year for my birthday. Feeling the weight of the steel immediately makes me feel safer.

With a weapon in each hand, I back down the path. When I'm positive nothing is following me, I spin around and stare into the yellow eyes of a huge tan cat. The gorgeous creature almost seems unreal with its perfect markings. Tan, slender body, eyes rimmed in thick black lines, and very sharp fangs.

A Florida panther.

I freeze in my spot and keep my breath shallow. No fast movements. No extra noise.

The animal growls again. This time, the sound is followed by a series of snarls and hisses. An awful sound that makes me want to cover my ears.

I keep my head down, but don't dare take my eyes off the wild animal. Partly because it's beautiful and partly because it's endangered.

But mostly, because it's about to attack.

The panther gives me a low warning and flattens its ears against its round shaped head.

Even though I'm stuck in some weird standoff with a

large and very dangerous feline...oddly, I still feel slightly relieved.

Besides an alligator, there's only one thing I'm afraid of running into.

More than an alligator.

More than this wild cat.

The thing I'm most afraid of these days is Al Smith.

SURVIVAL SKILL #1

We can judge the heart of a man by his treatment of animals.

Days earlier...

"Wake up."

The crackly voice pulls me from a deep sleep. When my eyes flutter open, Birdee's African Gray parrot perches on my chest.

He bends down and pecks the tip of my nose. Then the little bird squawks in my face. "Wake up!"

I groan and swing my pillow at the annoying avian. "Go away, Petey."

"I live here." The strange bird—that miraculously speaks in full sentences—bites my hand and flies away.

"Ouch!" I jolt upright, rubbing the spot he attacked for no reason. "Stupid bird."

Then I hear a faint "stupid bird" repeated in the hallway as Petey flees my wrath.

"Run, yah chicken!" I scream back, half-laughing.

"Someday I'm going to pluck you and make myself a nice, new pillow. No one will ever know."

"Danger!" The bird sings and flies off, most likely to find his master.

"Tattletale!" I yell after him. The fact that I'm arguing with and threatening a silly bird is totally embarrassing. I don't know why I let Petey get to me.

I roll out of bed, force my feet into my bear slippers, and drag myself down to the empty kitchen. I grab a blueberry pop tart and nibble a couple bites before heading outside, wondering where Birdee is this early.

Blocking my eyes from the blazing sun with my hand, I scan the back yard. It's only eight in the morning and it's already sticky. My pajamas cling to my skin. The warm breeze makes the temperature slightly more bearable, not quite hotter than hell...yet.

At the far end of the yard, a straw hat bobs through the green palm fronds.

Oh good, Birdee's on a mission. Distracted.

I crouch and sneak along the fence, obscured by bushes. I've only been living with my grandmother in the Everglades for over a month now, yet—as always—I still can't sneak up on her without being busted first. My dad was just like her.

Keen as a coon dog but mad as a hatter.

Slinking along the border of the yard, I hide behind a spiky palm tree and wait a few seconds before peeking out.

Birdee stands on the path, holding camo binoculars up to her eyes. She's looking directly above her, almost tilting way back.

I tiptoe closer—the closest I've gotten to date—putting one slipper in front of the other. This time I might just make it. Or so I think.

Until a feathered look-out flies over my head and squawks, "Intruder."

Birdee swings her binocular in my direction and laughs when she sees me in the lenses. "Ah ha! Thanks, Petey."

"Hey!" I pick up a pebble and launch it in the air at him, purposely missing. "Big mouth."

He darts out of the way and squawks back, "You throw like a girl."

Somehow, this dang bird outwits me, every single time. If I could catch him, I'd shove him in his cage for a few minutes. Without Birdee knowing. Maybe he'd finally accept that he's not human, he's a freakin' bird. Doesn't help that Birdee treats him like her little child.

My grandmother comes over and pats my shoulder. "Looks like we gotcha again, Chicken."

"We?" The nickname makes me smile, but I follow up with an overdramatic groan. "When do you have time to teach him that stuff?"

"When you're asleep…" Birdee turns her head and winks at me. "Which is quite a lot lately. You teens sure get tired doing nothing. Thought you were going to help me feed the animals this morning."

Behind us, the goats baa and the chickens cackle in protest at my lack of helping.

"Sorry. I guess the heat's getting to me." I wipe my face with the sleeve of my pajama shirt and jog a few steps to catch up as she walks toward the house. For an old woman with a hip replacement, she sure can move. "And I thought North Carolina had awful heat in the summer; this place is ten times worse than Hades. Please tell me it cools off some? Before winter?"

"It's cooler in the swamps." Birdee removes her hat and wipes her forehead with the purple handkerchief that always hangs from her back pocket. A glint flashes in her eyes, telling me she's in a teasing mood. "You should try it out there. Nice hike."

"Uh, no thanks." I make a face. "Maybe I forgot to mention that I'm severely and hyper allergic to alligators...actually, to all things that eat humans."

She waves me off. "Hm. These alligators ain't any worse than those bears you used to hang out with."

Before Dad died, I spent my life hiking in the Smokies with him, tagging bears and patrolling the woods for illegal hunters and greedy poachers. But alligators are on a whole other level.

"No thanks. I'll take my chances with big furry things over snapping death machines any day."

"Well then, enjoy the looooong hot summer." Birdee snaps her head up and puts a finger to her lips. "Shhhhhh!"

She scans the sky with her binoculars pressed to her face. No matter how old this woman gets, her spirit seems to grow younger and younger. Soon, she'll catch up with me.

I stare out at the beginning of the Cypress National Park that borders Birdee's property. Tall grass sways and the frogs sing in the breeze. A few egrets burst out of the trees and fly overhead. My grandmother likes to 'live on the edge,' as they say. Her home is the only private residence that backs up to the Cypress National Park. Only she calls it 'her backyard.' Not only is she neighbors with Mother Nature, but she has a menagerie of animals. Her goats and chickens provide milk and eggs, but there have been others that she rescues from time to time. Turtles, birds, deer, mice, and frogs have all called Birdee's place 'home'.

No wonder Dad loved it here so much.

There's no way to get any closer to nature than to hang out at Birdee's.

She gasps behind me, ripping me from my thoughts. "Well, butter my butt and call me a biscuit."

My stomach growls on cue, anticipating Birdee's homemade breakfast. I slap my tummy and keep my voice low, "What is it?"

"Look." She hands me the binoculars and points up to the robin-egg blue sky. "A bald eagle."

I look through the lenses, scanning the sky, barely dotted with wisps of clouds. "Where? I don't see it."

She repositions my head to the right a little. "There. Sitting in the top of that tree. Probably has some little eaglets. This is hatching season, you know."

I finally find the large bird in the viewer. Perched high in his home, glancing down at us. A few seconds later, he flies off.

I sigh after only catching a brief glimpse. Hardly an encounter. "Oh well, he's gone."

"Keep your eye out. Probably see him flying back and forth to the nest, bringing food to his lady friend. As it should be." She smiles and winks again.

We stand there watching the sky for several minutes until the eagle flies back to the nest with a fish dangling from his beak.

"I'm hungry," Petey squawks.

I keep my eye on the nest. "Birdee, do eagles eat African Grays, by chance?" Then I mumble under my breath, "Should I be so lucky."

Petey flies up into the palm tree. "Danger!"

"Chicken, stop teasing." Birdee playfully slaps my shoulder. "Don't scare him, now he'll never come down from there. Poor thing."

"Oh Lord." I shake my head and hand her the bird watching tool. "That bird gets more love than I do."

"That's not true. Yet." Birdee lets the binoculars hang from her neck and studies me. "Wait a minute...you sound grumpy. Have you eaten breakfast?"

"Couple bites of pop tart." I plaster on my most pitiful face.

"Good heavens, child. You're probably starving." She wraps one arm around my shoulders and leads me toward the door. "I haven't either so it's a date. Petey can eat later."

The little bird squawks from high in the tree. "Traitor."

"It's about time." I actually turn and smile up at the little bird, just to point out that I won this round. Fair and square. I walk inside, cursing myself. This bird probably has no clue about our rivalry and most likely doesn't even care. This is what I get for being an only child...endless bickering with a feathered sibling.

Birdee and I link arms as we walk into the house. She explains a few more facts about the eagle's nesting habits while I keep an eye out for Petey. The bird could be planning a pecking mission, out for his revenge.

Birdee bangs around the kitchen, and within record time, the room smells like bacon and egg biscuits. It's like the woman snaps her fingers and yummy food appears out of the humid air.

I start some fresh coffee and set the table with paper plates and mugs.

When I'm about to sit down, the front screen door opens.

Surely she didn't teach the bird to open the door.

Instead of chirps, a deep voice calls out, "Hoe gaan dit?"

"Hey Rex! We're in the kitchen," Birdee hollers.

I tickle her sides. "Your boyfriend is here."

"I told you, he's not my boyfriend." She pushes my hands away and refuses to make eye contact. "Just *friends with benefits*."

"Ahhh!" I jam my pointer fingers in both ears. "I'm going to pretend I didn't hear that."

"Hey, can't work all the time." Birdee straightens her apron and whispers in my direction, "A woman's gotta play."

"Stop, have mercy!" We both laugh as I set another plate for Rex to join us.

Birdee's "object of affection"—or whatever she calls him —pops his head around the corner. "Hallo."

Rex takes off his baseball hat, revealing thin white hair, and beelines for Birdee. "Hallo, mooi een!" He kisses the top of her hand like men did in the old days.

"Hi yourself." She swats his butt with a towel.

I groan. "Please! Get a room!"

Birdee and Rex both giggle like school kids.

"Goeie môre, Grace." Rex comes over and kisses my forehead. His white goatee scratches my skin.

I smile and repeat the Afrikaans greeting, minus the cool South African accent, plus my deep southern one. "Goeie môre."

Even though I've only known Rex a short time, he already feels like family. I never knew my grandfather; he died when I was young. So having Rex is a total bonus, and seeing Birdee happy makes me adore him even more. The two met in Africa after Dad died last year. She went there after the funeral to escape the pain of losing her only son. To pass the time, she ended up helping out on Rex's family's animal reserve.

After she returned, Rex showed up a few months later with his nephew to visit. They've been "visiting" Florida ever since, though I'm pretty sure they both have made it a permanent address. Rex bought a houseboat for him and his nephew, Dylan, to fix up. While Dylan works as an alligator wrestler at Alligator Land, Rex runs airboat tours for all the tourists. He says it's to make extra money, but since he's here all the time, I think it's an excuse to stay close to Birdee. Only I guess I've been cramping their 'friendship' for the last month or so while Mom hangs back in North Carolina, selling the house.

So we can start over.

Though I'm not sure that's what I want. I don't want to forget Dad and everything we had together there. The family. The house. The memories.

But Mom says 'we' needs a fresh start.

I kinda wish things could stay the same, but teens never get a say in any important matter. Instead, parents drag us around and make the decisions they think are *best* for us.

When really, it's better for them.

To me, relocating to Florida doesn't make the pain of losing Dad any less. It just moves the pain further south. To a different place with different memories and a different house.

Birdee places a heaping plate of food in front of me and a platter of biscuits in the middle of the table.

Rex leans over and sniffs the bread's mouth-watering perfume. "Hmmmm mmmmm! You know the way to an old man's heart, Miss Birdee."

"Your heart is in your stomach?" I ask.

"Close enough." Rex reaches over to snatch a biscuit off the steaming plate, but Birdee smacks the top of his hand. "Excuse me! Can we say grace first?"

He yanks his napkin into his lap and whispers to me, pretending Birdee can't hear. "I like a bossy woman." Rex bows his head and squeezes his eyes shut. "*Grace.* Good, now let's eat."

"I'm serious, Rex Kruger." Birdee sits down and throws a biscuit at his head.

He ducks as it lands on the counter and I laugh. "Rex, I wouldn't push her. Next, it'll be a knife or fork."

"Bring it on. I like a little sass."

Birdee playfully holds up a fist and shakes it in his face. "Don't make me hurt you."

"Might be fun." Rex kisses Birdee's cheek. Her face lights up like a tacky Christmas sweater.

I stop chewing and stare at them. "Seriously, you guys need to stop with the excessive PDA."

"We may be old..." Birdee says and winks at Rex.

He jumps in and follows her lead. "But we ain't dead yet."

She pours him some coffee and slides her napkin into her lap, which reminds me to do the same. "Oh Chicken, I almost forgot. Your mother called this morning. She got an offer on the house and hopes to close soon. She plans to come down in a few days."

I stop chewing. The biscuit quickly dries out in my mouth. "You think it'll really sell?"

Birdee glances at Rex and then focuses on me. "Looks like it."

None of us says another word.

I suddenly lose my whole appetite. Even for Birdee's delicious biscuits.

I keep my head down and try not to let my feelings overflow. Don't know why I'm upset; I knew this was coming. Shouldn't be a surprise. I guess I didn't think it'd sell so soon. Our town has been struggling to prosper for years. Businesses have closed, people have gone bankrupt. It's the main reason Carl got involved with the poaching ring in the first place—to help finance a dying town.

After all that, I assumed the house would stay on the market for a while. Definitely more than a month.

Now, not only is Dad gone, but now my home is almost gone too.

Ever since Al disappeared except for the random sightings around North Carolina, Mom decided it was best if we moved away. Even though no threat has ever been made, she thinks Al wants revenge against me for messing up his bear-poaching scheme. Whether she's right or not, I assume he's not thrilled I was indirectly involved with his stepsister, Katie's, untimely death. Though neither one was really my fault. He was illegally killing bears to make money, and she was killing wolves for a real estate deal.

No matter the reason, he probably blames me for both anyway.

Then again, no one has heard from Al since he escaped the Feds and fled the Smokies.

"Don't you think we could go home now? Before she sells?" I clear my throat, not sure if I believe what I'm saying. "Al hasn't been spotted in months."

"Sweeney figures as long as you stay down here, Al won't ever find you. The deed to this place is under my mom's maiden name. So you're much safer here. In North Carolina, you're trapped, like a cricket in a slippery bucket."

And she's right.

I do feel safe here. Normal. I just wish the fear hanging over our heads—whether real or not—didn't cost Mom the family home.

Even though Sweeney offered protection, Birdee made it clear that she didn't want the police hanging around her home. But Mo and Sweeney promised me they would always have someone close by, keeping an eye on us in the background. Just in case Al pops up on the radar again. I had to promise not to let Birdee know.

"What she don't know won't piss her off." Sweeney had said.

And I've never said a thing. No use worrying her or Mom.

Sometimes, in the grocery store, I find myself looking, hoping to discover who it is. Wishing it was secretly Mo so I could see him more. Not knowing kinda makes it all a little creepier.

Birdee clears her throat. When I look at her, she eyes my plate.

I force myself to smile and take a bite.

Rex watches me too, never saying a word. He knows the whole story, but he'd never jump in, comment, or take sides. And if he did, I'm pretty sure he'd go with Birdee or he'd probably end up "enemies with no benefits."

I stare at my plate and poke a piece of gristle. "Did anyone else call?"

"Mo hasn't called sweetie," Birdee says matter-of-factly. Like it's no big deal.

"Oh," I mumble as my heart sinks.

I haven't seen my boyfriend since he drove me down here six weeks ago. Doesn't seem fair. After being apart and thinking he was dead, we finally reunite, only to be separated once again. This time the distance is much longer and much harder. It's been barely a month, but somehow it feels like a whole year. Thank goodness for the one picture I have of us, or I'm pretty sure I'd forget what he looked like. Though his hotness will never be forgotten.

To make things worse, Sweeney forbids us from talking too, making sure no one tracks me here.

"But he will, I promise." She reaches over and cups my hand. "I know this is hard on you, Chicken. But things will fall into place very soon, I promise."

Tears sting my eyes as everything mushes together. I miss Mom, and the thought of getting rid of Dad's house is almost unbearable. That house is all we have left of him. Of us as a family. Without it, he's gone and our family is forever changed. Not that's it's the same.

To make things even worse, not seeing or even talking to Mo is horribly painful. And in my mind, everything—this whole mess—is my fault. If I hadn't gotten obsessed with finding Dad, tracking those poachers, and taking down Al, maybe we'd all be together now. If I hadn't realized Katie, Al's stepsister, was part of a real estate conspiracy that caused the deaths of many endangered red wolves, maybe none of this would have ever happened.

Maybe then, Dad would be alive. My family would be safe. Mo and I would be together.

And my ongoing nightmare about Al finding me would finally go away.

Then again, maybe not.

Rex jumps in and breaks the awkward silence. "How about we take the boat out? We can fish. Get some peace and quiet."

"You're not working today?" Birdee asks.

He shrugs. "It's Sunday. I don't have anyone booked. Can't imagine going out on the water without taking my two favorite ladies. Dylan can come too."

Birdee squeezes my hand. "That sounds fun. Doesn't it, Chicken?"

I nod as I make my cold eggs skate in figure eights around my plate, "Sure, why not?"

I haven't been fishing in a long time. And even though I won't be flyfishing, maybe getting out on the water will lift my spirits.

It always has in the past.

Then again, floating in alligator-infested sludge is not my idea of peaceful.

SURVIVAL SKILL #2

Going swimming in alligator infested waters is just plain stupid.

Riding in an airboat feels like flying.

Now I know what an egret feels like.

As the airboat races through Cypress National Park, I push the plugs further into my ears, hoping to muffle the loud sounds of the raging engine.

Rex sits high in the captain's chair and yells out facts every now and then. Birdee rides next to him, holding onto her straw hat. A huge grin slices her face in half as the wind whips through her hair.

Rex's nephew, Dylan, sits next to me on the plastic seat. Every now and then, he jabs my ribs with his sharp elbow and points out a spectacular sight. This is the most time I've spent with Dylan since I moved down here. He's usually working at Alligator Land, and I'm usually home with the birds.

I rub my side, convinced I'll have a big bruise tomorrow. Dylan doesn't realize how strong he is. Sitting next to him now, I can't help but notice that his biceps are as almost twice as big as my thighs. A modern day Paul Bunyan, complete with checkered shirt and bulging muscles. In place of an ax to cut down trees, Dylan carries a machete to slice through thick vegetation. He doesn't have a blue ox, but he does drive a junky blue truck that makes weird noises.

So I'd say they're even.

None of us can hear a thing over the howling wind. But to be honest, the Everglades need no words, no explanation. The view says it all. Loud and clear. There's no mistaking the voice of the Everglades. Nothing like it in the whole world. Unfortunately, as much as I want to enjoy this side trip and simply revel in the beauty of this wonderland, something is always missing.

Mo.

I can't help but wish he were here so I could share all this with him.

When he's not around, no matter how bright the sun or how sparkling the water, my world seems a little dimmer.

I close my eyes and let the warm rays kiss my face, hoping to boil my good spirits back up to the surface. The cool breeze masks the blazing heat.

We buzz around a sharp corner and head into a waving field of floating saw grass. Cute little pink spoonbills and a family of white Ibis hear the boat and lift off to safety. A few pelicans glide above us, maintaining their V formation. No matter what goes on below, they hold their course.

I could learn a thing or two from them.

Rex slows down the boat, giving my deafened ears a rest.

I pull out one earplug and hear his voice over the puttering engine. "The Cypress National Park is nearly 750,000 acres of gorgeous. Amazing, isn't it?"

Birdee grips her straw hat with both hands and screams over the noise. "Been here twenty years and it still gets to me." Her eyes glisten with moisture and I'm not sure if it's tears from the wind or the wild.

Dylan elbows me again. "How many times a day do you

think he rattles off that fact?" His accent is not nearly as thick as Rex's. Almost sounds American unless you listen close enough.

I shrug. "He's just trying to impress his little love bird."

I watch Birdee laugh with Rex. They hold hands as he drives. I can't help but smile when I'm around them. Rex is completely in love with Birdee, even more than he is with the Everglades. Which says a lot. And I don't blame him. She's a special lady.

There's only one Birdee in the world. That's for sure.

Dylan tightens the short blonde ponytail at the base of his neck.

I give it a tug. "How long you gonna let this thing grow?"

He shrugs and his caterpillar eyebrows raise higher on his forehead. "Going for Brad Pitt's look in The Counselor. Got him some chicks."

"Yeah, good luck with that." I nod once and have to hold back from sputtering with laughter. Dylan could probably pull off a Brad Pitt impression if he was fifty pounds lighter and five inches shorter. The guy has a better chance of stardom by fighting in the WWF.

In the background, Rex continues blurting out Everglade facts from the Frommer's Guide like we've paid for his official airboat tour. He'll probably charge me twenty bucks if I listen too carefully. His accent jumbles every few words, but I get the gist. "Most people think this place is a huge swamp but we've got more than that. Hammocks, pinelands, prairies, marshes. A real smorgasbord of beauty. Where else can we get so many different terrains?"

We? I mouth to Dylan.

Rex thinks he is the swamp and the swamp is he.

Dylan rolls one finger close to his head. Rex is crazy, which is what makes me like him so much more.

Birdee turns around and catches us. She gives us a dirty

look and shakes her finger, warning me to behave. As quickly as it appears, the frown drops off her face and she smiles up at Rex again. "I love how much you know about this place."

"I love you." Rex says back and kisses her cheek.

Behind her back, I mouth *told yah* to Dylan. *Love birds.*

As Rex woos Birdee with his statistics and knowledge of the unique ecosystem, I glance out over the glistening surface. The watery fields of floating saw grass—that Rex calls the River of Grass—stretch as far as I can see.

I can't help but smile.

Dad loved it here. Before he died, we visited several times a year. He pretended it was to see his mother, but I know the truth. He loved the Glades. Then again, he loved anything green and grassy. But whenever we came to visit Birdee, Dad always left here changed.

Refreshed. Recommitted to nature. Revived.

The Everglades does that to you.

Rex leans over and kisses the top of Birdee's hat. I'm pretty sure Dad would have loved him the way I do. Because I've never seen Birdee happier than when Rex is around. Though she wouldn't admit her secret to save a snail.

I hope someday I can see Mom happy again too.

Dylan yells at his uncle. "Hey! Speaking of *smorgasbord,* it's time to eat!"

Rex nods and swerves down a less-traveled water highway until he comes to a complete stop. The boat goes from loud to silent in a matter of seconds. In the distance, a symphony of birds plays. A small cane patch whistles as a few birds caw and cackle their backup tunes. The water softly sloshes as it lightly strums the riverbanks. The boat floats closer to some tall reeds and cattails.

I scoot away from the boat's edge when one brushes my shoulder. "Here?" I peer over the edge and push away the thick vegetation that's already trying to climb up the side.

"Shouldn't we head toward land or maybe out in the middle?" Because in my mind, why hover in areas where animals like to hide?

I love nature and all. But the last thing I want is to have a staring contest with an American alligator that's only interested in winning a side helping of human.

"Good a place as any." Rex tosses me a sandwich. "Cream cheese and olives with extra garlic salt."

I grab it and grin. "Just how I like it."

"Dylan, go long." Rex throws another Ziploc bag over my head. Dylan tries to grab the end but it bounces off the deck and flies overboard, landing in the swampy water.

I laugh and hang over the side. The sandwich floats in the water a few feet below us. "That sucks, and I'm not sharing." I lick my sandwich and take a bite, chewing dramatically.

"Gross." Dylan groans and watches his floating lunch. "Man, you need to work on your passes."

"Hey I'm old, not my fault. Next time...*dive.*"

"No worries! If that kinda bag can keep my phone dry, pretty sure the sandwich won't drown either." Dylan removes his t-shirt, revealing a white tank. An alligator claw hangs from a leather string around his neck. Not sure if it's jewelry or his weapon of choice. He climbs past me and hangs over the side of the boat. His hand grazes the water and his fingertips touch the bag's edge.

For a few seconds, I hold my breath, eyeing the glassy surface. I find myself searching for bubbles or ripples or extra big teeth. You could not pay me enough money to hang over reptile-infested water for a freakin' roast beef sandwich.

Dylan grabs the Ziploc.

Out of nowhere, the water explodes as an alligator launches itself from the reeds. He snaps his jaws closed, barely missing Dylan's hand.

Obviously caught off guard, Dylan yells and loses the bag

as the alligator drops back in the water, landing with a huge splash. "Whoa!"

"Jeez," I hear myself mutter as I sink back into my chair.

Rex calls out, laughing. "Ha! Told you it was a good sandwich."

"Goodness gracious! That was close." Birdee moves next to me and protectively grips my shoulders with both hands, yanking me into her. "Mary would kill me if anything happened to you. I promised her I'd watch you like a duck on a June bug."

"I'm fine." I say, my hands tremble slightly in my lap. I glance over the edge, waiting for the alligator to make an encore. The once-still water ripples with waves. "Dylan's the crazy one."

"Man. Didn't even see that sucker coming. I'm off my game."

"Game?" I ask. "Looks like you almost lost."

Dylan stands on the edge and stares at the water. The baggie floats a few feet away, stuck in a clump of grass. "Nope. Stupid gator missed. And he didn't even get the bag. Think he's still there?"

"Don't do it Dylan. Not worth it." Rex calls out, obviously amused. "You can eat Birdee's carrots and celery. Though she probably won't share her ranch dressing. Take it from me. Just let the gator have it."

"Over my dead body." Without warning, Dylan dives into the water like a seal.

"Dylan!" I jump up and grip the railing, searching the water for him.

Birdee yells up at Rex. "He's gonna end up that alligator's lunch if you don't do something!"

"Dylan's fine." He shakes his head. "Does it every day. This is just his off-the-job training."

Birdee and I hold hands, carefully watching the water.

Waiting for him to surface.

"Do you see him?" I holler.

Rex scans the marshes and then takes another bite of his sandwich. "Nope. Not yet. Give him a minute."

"A minute? How is he so calm?" I ask.

"Because sometimes he's a camel's ass?" She says it loud enough for Rex to hear.

"Aren't we testy?" The smile on Rex's face dims and he sits back down in the captain's seat without another word and continues eating. "He's fine. Trust me."

For a second, everything is quiet. The birds have stopped singing. A turtle that's been sunbathing on a log remains frozen. He's not going in the water any time soon.

Even he thinks Dylan is nuts.

Suddenly, Dylan bursts out of the water, holding the gator by the tail. "I got him!"

Instead of thinking *Thank God*, the only word that comes to mind is *dumbass*.

"Whoa, Junior! That's gotta be a twelve-footer," Rex stands and holds out his hands as if measuring. "Small potatoes, if you ask me. Half the size of those monsters they got you wrestling down there."

"Shoot. You get in here, ole man." Dylan breathes heavy as he thrashes along with the gator, who is probably confused at the new odd species invading his territory.

After getting a good grip, Dylan clamps the alligator's mouth shut and holds him out of the water. "Grace, you want some new shoes?"

I shake my head at the bad joke. He may laugh but I know that alligator boots are still in style and go for a good $1,000. "Put it back. Poor thing. You're terrorizing him in his own home."

"Dylan! Shame on you!" Birdee yells. "This is not funny. Not one bit."

"Sorry Miss Birdee. I was just kidding."

She puts her hands on her hips and towers over him. "Fine, then stop showing off."

Dylan releases his opponent. The poor reptile, now a total embarrassment in the gator community, zooms off as fast as his tail will allow. He knows he's met his match.

A sun lovin' alligator wrestler who's obviously much hungrier than any alligator.

Dylan watches as his opponent retreats and then slogs toward the reeds in the chest-high water until he reaches the sandwich. He grabs the bag and waves it in the air like it's a lasso. "Got it!"

"Good boy!" Rex yells down.

"Dylan Kruger. You get up here this instant unless you want me to wrestle you out of there myself." Birdee stands with her hands on her hips and taps her foot impatiently. "Now…before you give me a heart attack. I'm an old woman, yah know."

While they kid around, I hold my breath and watch the water. One of these gators is sure to come back and defend his friend. My hands are balled into tight fists and my muscles are squeezed tight.

Rex takes off his hat and wipes his brow. "Oh get off his case. Dylan's a top alligator wrestler. To him, playing with alligators is about as dangerous as swatting gnats."

"Rex! I don't care." Birdee shoots her eye darts at him instead. "We will talk about this later."

He bows and slips his hat back on his head. "I look forward to it."

Birdee can't help but smile. She's turned into a big softie.

Rex hollers down at Dylan. "The Love Boat is about to leave son, so I suggest you climb aboard quickly."

Dylan swims to the boat and tosses the sandwich onto the

deck. He grips the ledge and launches himself out of the water into the boat. "Ah! The water's perfect."

As soon as his body clears the river, I exhale and relax, careful not to let him see how scared I really was.

"Jerk." As soon as he's safe, I punch him in the arm, which probably hurts as much as a gnat gnawing on an elephant's backside. But I don't know what else to do with the adrenaline surging through my veins. And since I'm not great at expressing myself well, physical abuse seems appropriate, given the situation.

"I knew what I was doing." Dylan's massive muscles gleam with the swampy water. I can see why the alligator was scared. He'd probably break a tooth after chomping down on this hunk of meat.

"Whatever." I throw a towel at him hard. My weapon of choice. "Put some clothes on."

As Dylan towels off and pulls on a shirt, I mutter loud enough for him to hear. "No sane person swims with a gator for a stupid sandwich."

"I beg to differ." When I turn around, Dylan opens the bag and holds it up. "It's *roast beef.*"

"Sure it's funny now, until someone loses a limb. You could have been killed."

"But I wasn't." Dylan smiles and takes a bite of bread, all cocky-like. Water drips off his blonde hair into a puddle at his feet.

Birdee clicks her tongue. "You wait 'til I tell your girlfriend about this. Disrupting protected waters, touching a protected species— all for processed meat full of nasty preservatives."

Dylan's face drops. "You wouldn't."

"I would and I will." Birdee crosses her arms in defiance. "Sadie will set this right."

I smile at the threat.

From what I hear, Sadie will not be happy. I haven't met her yet but I look forward to it after hearing what a tough girl she is. Evidently tougher than me.

Rex laughs from the top of the boat. "Dylan's more afraid of his girlfriend and an old bird than a hungry alligator."

"He should be," Birdee says and winks at me.

SURVIVAL SKILL #3

When hiking at night, you will hear the sounds of nocturnal animals, so make sure you are prepared for them.

After scouring the Everglades for new and exciting things until dusk, Rex finally turns the boat around. The motor sputters as we swerve along the winding water-ways. Glowing eyes dot the water as alligators surface to investigate the disturbance. Either that or they're plotting revenge for the earlier attack on their brother and his lunch prey.

I keep an eye out for other animal sightings. They are all around, but you can only see them if you focus. I spot a cottonmouth snake slipping into the water and watch a great blue heron stalk fish in the shallow water like a true pro. The day's sounds disappear as the night sky fills with a new lullaby. Frogs, crickets, and birds with the occasional blood-curdling growl.

"What is that strange noise?" I search the tree line as we near the dock.

"Everglades' pride and joy." Rex slows the boat down until it chut-chutters along. "Florida panther."

"Otherwise known as the cougar," says Dylan.

Birdee pipes up too. "Or puma."

"A lot of aliases for a big cat." I grab Birdee's binoculars and scan the woods even though it's too dark to make out anything. "I thought they were extinct?"

"Endangered." Dylan corrects. "There are only about one hundred and fifty in the wild."

"And they're all right here. Lucky us." Rex stops the boat and lets the motor idle. I scan the horizon, searching for a flash of yellow or tan. "We could probably grow the population if it wasn't for those poachers and roadside zoos. The fast cars racing down county roads like it's the Daytona 500 don't help."

"Aw, that's sad." I think about the red wolves from this past winter. Despite my efforts, they still can't seem to grow their numbers or families safe in the wild. I found several dead last year. Sounds like Florida panthers are the red wolves of the south.

Birdee nods. "So many animals to save. Not enough people to help."

Rex gives me a few minutes to look around. My eyes strain to see in the dimming light. Once it's obvious no panther will make an appearance, Rex moves the boat and heads back to the dock.

When we reach the platform, Dylan jumps out and grabs a rope to tie us up. The guy is a regular cowboy of the Everglades.

Rex helps Birdee out of the boat, and I climb down after them.

Dylan walks over when he's done wrangling the ship, clapping dirt off his hands. "Ready to go?"

The four of us walk down the path toward Birdee's house. For older people, Birdee and Rex walk much faster. Either Rex is hungry due to his never-ending appetite, or Dylan is slow due to his abnormal size.

Dylan and I hang back a little and chat as Rex and Birdee walk hand-in-hand down the path.

He rambles on about alligator wrestling and boasts about his alligator encounters in the wild, resulting in the alligator claw around his neck. His pride and joy.

I respond with a few "hmmms" and "ohhhs" but can't seem to focus on what he's saying. Even though the day's heat has crashed my brain, my nerves ramp up. Long shadows grow and blend into the evening dark, catching my attention. I get the strange feeling something—or someone—is watching me.

Every few feet, I glance back into the Cypress National Park, scanning the bushes. It's nice living along the edge of the wild swamps, among the purest nature around. However, I'm always on guard. On alert. Unable to relax. Being in unfamiliar territory is unsettling. In the mountains, I can name every bend, every rock, every creek.

Here, every sound and sight still feels new.

Having a psycho on the loose doesn't help things much. If they could catch Al, most of my fear would probably go away. Forever.

I notice how the tops of the palms sway in the warm breeze. One of the things I miss most from home is the scent of pine when the wind blows. The clear rivers—so clean you can drink from them. The fishing holes, clear and sparkling.

Here, the air is humid and sticky. The water, a whole different experience. Murky and dangerous.

Off to my right, the tall grass sways, causing me to stop and focus.

A flash of yellow catches my eye and a low growl rides the wind. "Did you hear that?"

"No." Dylan stops and listens. Then he glances at his watch. "Oh crap, Sadie's going to kill me!"

"Why?"

He quickens his steps and speed walks past Rex. "I'm late for the protest."

Rex laughs. "Uh oh. Wouldn't want to be in your flip flops right now."

"Wait, what protest?" I ask, trying to catch up with him.

Dylan talks over his shoulder but doesn't turn around. He's on a mission. "My girlfriend is running a protest against a roadside zoo not far from here."

"Little 60s, isn't it?"

Dylan shrugs. "Sometimes the old way works better than the new one. People talk too much these days. Sadie does something about it. Wait, did I just say that?"

"Yes you did, and it's true." Rex playfully nudges Dylan. "Hey, why don't you take Grace? Bet she and Sadie would be a great team."

"That's a great idea," Birdee squeaks out. "It will do you good to get out. Hang out with kids your own age."

I shake my head. "Nah. I'll stay here with you guys. It's quiet."

"Too quiet—and since when do you like quiet, anyway?" Birdee puts both hands on her hips. "Nothing going on here to stay for. Boring old woman, a crazy bird, and dirty old man." She grins at Rex.

I throw my hands up. "I don't want to hear any more about what you old people do. Clean or dirty."

Rex and Dylan both laugh, but Birdee's face turns a shade pinker than usual. "Don't think you're too old for me to whoop on, Chicken."

I smile. "Hmmm. This protest is sounding better and better every minute."

We walk up the driveway. Rex and Birdee keep heading into the house while I follow Dylan to his truck.

He opens the driver's door. "Well? You coming?"

"Sure, why not?" I slip around the side and hop in the passenger seat. "You only live once."

"Ever been to a real protest?" Dylan asks as he backs the truck out of the driveway.

As he skids out onto the dirt road, I grab on to the handle for dear life. "Not an official one, with signs and stuff."

"Oh! You're in for a treat."

Sadie's protest is no small potatoes.

When we pull up, camera vans and crews line the road out. Local T.V. stations and media walk around interviewing people that are standing along the side spectating. For a small town, this is a big event.

Dylan beams and points through the window. "There she is."

A young, wiry girl with short spiky hair, dressed comfortably in a black tank top and black capris with purple Keens, stands next to a reporter in front of *Uncle Bob's Animal Park*. Sadie holds a homemade sign that says: **Ban Roadside Zoos!**

As we walk up, I stand on my tiptoes and try to see over the high fence. "What animals do they have in there?"

Dylan frowns. "Unfortunately, everything and anything."

By the time we reach Sadie, she's already mid-monologue.

"These animals are bought on the down-lo and shoved into small cages. They deserve a chance to live in their own habitat and have a happy life. The state of Florida needs to ban these pop-up roadside zoos or enforce regulations to ensure they are a proper facility for these animals."

I like this girl. As I watch her discuss regulations and laws, I must say I'm totally impressed. "She sounds super smart."

"Too smart. She graduated this year with straight A++. Wants to study environmental science. Hopes to go off to UF next year."

"Why not this fall, then?" I ask.

"She's taking a year off to 'make a difference.' At least that is what she says. Her dad's wealthy so she can afford to hang back at home."

I study this girl. She has an assortment of beads wrapped around her wrist and a small nose ring. A fringed backpack hangs off her back. Looks more hippie rebel than geeky scientist.

Dylan throws out another nugget. "He's the mayor of Homestead. Pro big biz all the way."

"And what does daddy say about his openly protesting conservationist daughter fighting for a spot on the local news?"

"Oh she's definitely a daddy's girl." Dylan stands a few feet back and tries to catch Sadie's eye. When she seem him, she smiles wide but keeps talking. "She can do no wrong and he would do anything for her. Though he usually stays away from these kinds of things."

Explains the excessive media coverage.

I watch as Sadie moves from reporter to reporter. Every time she laughs, she touches the reporter's shoulder. Anyone can tell that they all love her. "With her family connections, it shouldn't be hard to get a few laws changed here and there."

"Yeah? That's probably the one thing they don't agree on. He's more about big business. She's more about the little four-legged guy."

I cringe at the thought of being on opposite sides of the fence with your family. Dad and I were always on the same side with everything. "Must suck."

"She doesn't care, she just keeps at it." Dylan grabs

another sign that reads: **Keep the Wild in the Wild. Close Uncle Bob's!**

I keep up the pace next to him as he moves through the crowd. "How does she feel about you working at Alligator World?"

"I'm the least of her worries." Dylan says, "Besides, my work there is to help teach people that alligators aren't monsters."

"Looks like you like to teach alligators a little something about humans too."

He smiles. "Do me a favor and not mention that thing today, or Sadie will jump on my case instead of Bob's."

"Your attack on a poor helpless animal is safe with me." He laughs as I zip my mouth.

We wait along the sidelines as Sadie converses with a Channel 8 reporter who launches into some statistics. "In the United States, there are thousands of roadside zoos. While there are some regulations, they are very limited and vary by state. Here at *Uncle Bob's* there are over fifty wild animals, including tigers, wolves, and even a few ligers - an unnatural breed between male lions and female tigers. This pairing creates a huge problem that weighs more than 1,000 pounds."

The reporter cuts to a cage with a massive liger, twice the size of a Siberian tiger. Sitting, his massive head is as tall as mine. I bet he'd reach ten feet tall if he stood up on his hind legs.

I can't stop staring. "Wow. Wouldn't want to see that in the wild."

Dylan keeps his voice low. "Yeah, but it's sad. These animals are freaks. Nowhere would a tiger and lion breed. These crappy animal parks are going rampant in Florida and are doing whatever it takes to get some kind of show. Who knows how many other states have them?"

I think of the bear pits in North Carolina and how hard Dad tried to shut them down. Beautiful creatures stuck in small cages, living out their lives on concrete grass. There's been talk of closing them ever since Al and his buddies were caught in cahoots with their owner, Chief Reed, but I haven't seen anything done yet. I make a mental note to check in with Tommy for the status. I had no idea the problem was bad in other states.

Sadie's voice is loud compared to the noise around us. A few T.V. stations rush over and hang big fuzzy mics over her head. But she doesn't falter in the least.

Her voice is strong and solid. "Uncle Bob's Park has been cited by the U.S. Department of Agriculture for over 100 violations of the Animal Welfare Act. This includes citations for inadequate safety barriers and improper housing. Yet, this shithead just added two new tigers, a few extra bears, and is managed by a guy who displays tiger hides in his house. This abuse has to stop."

The reporter, who visibly cringed when Sadie cussed on camera, does a quick wrap-up and throws the story back to the studio. The reporter drops her smile and frowns at Sadie then packs up her gear. When she leaves, Sadie shoots her a bird.

I can't help but smile.

We need more Sadies in the world. To balance the Skylers.

I've never had many friends that were girls. Technically, Wyn doesn't count. Madison was okay, though we haven't talked since her family moved away from North Carolina immediately following the red wolf incident. They didn't seem to like me much anyway. For some reason, I've been labeled a troublemaker in my hometown. Which is frustrating because I actually try to prevent trouble from happening. It just doesn't seem to work very well.

My whole life I've had a hard time meeting girls I could relate to. While they were all off playing with dolls and dressing up, I was out getting dirty, hiking and fishing with Dad. My only consistent friend has been Wyn. Thinking of him makes me remember that my weekly Skype visit with him is tomorrow. Can't wait to tell him about the panther. Though I'm not crazy about hearing another drama story about Skyler, who after six months still leaves dumb notes in his locker and makes him CDs. I mean, who does that anymore? I don't know why she bothers me; she just does.

Once the cameras are turned off, Sadie approaches us with a big smile on her face.

"Lay one on me, yah big handsome man." She kinda sighs the last part and walks right up to Dylan, planting a big kiss on his lips. It's the first time I've seen him turn red from anything other than sunburn. I'm probably blushing too. Must be nice. They seem so confident in life and love.

Then Sadie turns to me and grins a dimpled smile. "You must be Grace." She practically jumps on me and gives me a huge hug like we've known each other forever. "Dylan's told me all about your kickass bear rescues and wolf conservation work. It's about time he let me meet you!" Then her huge smile flops into a deep frown and her brow deepens. "I'm sorry about your dad. And your friend, too."

"Thanks." I still can't forget Seth and the steep price he paid after saving me that awful winter night. If it wasn't for Seth and Wyn, I would have died. Most people who get sucked into snowdrifts are never seen again. Then images of Dad dying in my arms creep in. I push them away as a lump forms in my throat. "Me too."

Because what else can I say?

A short pudgy man stomps up the driveway with a shotgun in his hands. When he reaches the gate, he fires a shot in the air. We all duck and cover our ears. Instead of freezing like most of the crowd, I dive behind the van. I've heard enough gunshots in the last year to last me a lifetime and I know how things can turn bad...very quickly. Before you know what hits you.

"You're all trespassing on my land!" The man yells. "Gonna call the cops."

I peek out from behind the barrier to watch the showdown.

Sadie remains standing while everyone else cowers and speaks her mind. "This street is public property, *Bob*. We have a right to protest on public land, according to the First Amendment."

He points to a cameraman shooting footage over the fence. "He's on the line."

The news crew backs up.

"You afraid the news will see something?" Sadie asks and crosses her arms. "How horrible this place is? What you're doing to those animals?"

The man shakes a fist at her. "You're a pain in my ass, little girl. I suggest you pack up and go home or I'll..."

Instead of looking scared, she appears angry and takes a step toward him, standing her ground. "Is that a threat, Bobby?"

I don't know why, but this bold move forces me to come out from behind the van. Even though my legs are trembling, I walk over and stand next to Sadie in a united front.

Sadie smiles and points to all the news vans taping the confrontation. She clicks her tongue like a scolding parent. "Now, Bobby. And on T.V.? Not too smart if you ask me."

"I didn't." Bob zeroes in on my face and points with his gun. "You in on this too?"

I keep my eyes on him and refuse to look away in submission. "Yes."

"And me too." Dylan moves to Sadie other side. He

protectively stands there, but doesn't say anything else. He lets Sadie handle the dirty work. And why not? She's doing a great job on her own. She doesn't need a guy to rescue her.

Bob's face turns apple red. He shakes his gun at us. "You have ten minutes to clear this land before I call the police."

I want to say something, but after everything I've been through, I'm still damaged. Scared. Less than who I was. Standing here is about as much as I can do. Even that is tough. The last year has muted my voice and dulled my sharp tongue. I hope someday to get it back.

"Good! Call them." Sadie cranes her neck. "Because I'd love to see them search this place. Because surely you have the proper licenses and documentation for all your purchases and 'inventory' back there. Right?"

The man grits his teeth and spins on one heel, knowing he has lost this battle. He storms back in the house.

A few people slowly emerge from their hiding places like scared animals.

Sadie spins around and gives Dylan a kiss. "My hero."

"You don't need my saving, babe." Dylan picks her up and swings her around before setting her down gently. "Guess you told him."

"All in a day's work." She cocks her head as if she's studying me in a new light. "We're not so different, Grace. You and me. If we girls stick together, we could change the world."

It's the first time I see myself through someone else's eyes. Someone who sees me for who I am. Not who I was or what I did. Just me in this moment. Now.

For months, I've been blaming myself for Dad. For Carl. For Seth. Even for Katie, the woman who helped me in the red wolf investigation. Though she ended up being directly involved in the plot as well as Al's stepsister. Even though she killed herself, I still feel guilty.

Convinced I've done nothing but wrong. That everything that's happened has been for nothing. None of my sacrifices have mattered.

Yet, to Katie, I was a strong adversary. Not a weak opponent.

Maybe all along, I've been doing the right thing. The best way I knew how.

Maybe I'm looking at it in the wrong way.

Maybe I need a new view.

SURVIVAL SKILL #4

―――――――

Attempting to rescue a sick or injured mammal can be very dangerous.

After Bob goes inside, Dylan drives me back to Birdee's. Sadie talks the whole time. About her cause. About her plans. About how she hopes we made a difference today.

I used to think I was making a difference. Every day. But in the end, bears, wolves and people I cared about died for what now seems like nothing.

I glance out at the window and watch the palm trees pass us by.

Sadie rolls down her window and slings her feet out the side, wiggling her red-painted toes. "I guess we showed him."

I pull back my hair into a band to keep it from slapping my face. "He seemed madder than I expected."

She talks over her seat. "Criminals are never happy."

Dylan drives with one arm on the wheel and his other bent out his open window. The heat invades the truck's small space but the wind whips through the king cab adding a refreshing breeze. "What's your dad gonna say about this one?"

"Who cares?" Sadie barks. "The guy's housing *illegal* animals. Those poor things all deserve to be placed in some kind of sanctuary. This business of keeping animals in pens for humans to view and poke is absurd."

Dylan reaches over and strokes her hair. "She hates more than these roadside tourist traps. Sadie doesn't like anything —amusement parks, aquariums, circuses, or zoos."

"They all suck."

This surprises me. Since Dad was a forest ranger, I've grown up around preserving the woods and protecting animals against poaching. The roadside zoos around Cherokee were always a target, but I've never thought about official zoos or parks. "Aren't those more about teaching conservation?"

"Some have conservation in mind," Dylan says. "Alligator Land rescued our alligators."

"Seriously? Pul-ease. You know as well as I do, there is no proof those alligators were hurt or abandoned. You think they like living in cement pools?"

"Easy, tiger." Dylan cups her hand.

"Don't easy me! You don't want to admit it, but any place like Alligator Land contributes to the abuse of animals under the pretense of 'conservation.' She holds up her fingers in quotes on the last words. Then she pulls her feet inside and turns around in the seat to face me. "Have you heard about Sea World and what they do to those whales?"

I shake my head. I've lived in the forest bubble my whole life, so I haven't given much thought to anything beyond bears and the borders of North Carolina, but I've always been fascinated by whales and dolphins. It's my dream to work with them.

Dylan makes an 'I'm scared' face in the rear view mirror. He's obviously triggered something that is much deeper than Uncle Bob's.

"Or, did you know the Georgia Aquarium pays someone to capture beluga whales?" Sadie asks. "If we have to put animals in captivity—the ones that have been rehabilitated, not animal-napped—then we should build natural sanctuaries where animals can live out their lives in a dignified and peaceful way. People could still make money- I mean, who wouldn't pay to go see a bear or dolphin in a natural setting? Do we really need to see them perform stupid, humiliating tricks?"

I lean forward, amazed by her knowledge about these things. "I never thought of it that way."

"Well you better start if you hang out with me. Right, Dylan?" Dylan nods but doesn't' say a word as he drives. Probably scared to. "We've got Uncle Bob by the reproductive organs. His place won't stay open for long. Sea World is next on my shit list."

The girl has a list.

I think of Dad. He was always so active. Sometimes I wonder if I just get thrown into conservation. Nothing active about it. The issues pop up around me. Here's a girl who goes looking for things to fight for. Whereas, for the last six months, I've been looking for ways to stay away from anything that might be trouble. Maybe it's time to fight more for something I believe in. Instead of waiting for it to happen to me.

Dylan turns down Birdee's road and slows down when he reaches the first animal crossing sign. He rolls along past many more: turtles, deer, skunk; you name it, Birdee will think you should stop for it.

Out my window, a strange roar pierces the silence.

"Wait, stop!"

Dylan slams on the brake, probably assuming he's about to hit one of the animals Birdee's protecting. He knows she would have his hide if anything was hurt on her land.

I hang out my window. Sadie leans out the front and stares in the same direction. "What is it?"

"I heard something." I scan the trees, waiting to notice anything out of place.

Dylan lets the engine idle. "Newsflash. You always hear animal noises out here. What's the big deal?"

Sadie waves him off, ears alert. "Jesus. Turn off the car."

As soon as he cuts the engine, the noise sounds off again. It's closer than I thought.

"There. Did you hear it?" Sadie asks. She sits in her door window, feet on the seat and hands on top of the car.

Dylan scoffs. "Now, why would an animal be out here, in these parts? I mean, it's the Everglades."

Sadie kicks him through the window.

I open the car door, ears perked. "No. It sounded different than the calls I normally hear this time of day." I walk a few steps along the road, searching for the animal responsible.

Sadie jumps out after me, carrying her swamp boots. "Wait up!"

Dylan gets out of the car and leans against the truck. "Come on, girls. Don't get all Jane on me. It's an *animal*."

"It's a distressed animal, butthead. Can't you tell?"

Dylan pats the top of the car. "I love it when you talk dirty."

"Shut up." Sadie smiles and yanks on her shoes. Then she gives me a thumbs-up. "Grace is right. Something is hurt out here and needs our help."

The sound comes again, much louder this time.

"It's a freakin' cat." Sadie bolts off into the prickly brush and disappears.

Dylan jumps out of the car and storms after her. "Damn it, Sadie. I hate when you do this." The foliage swallows him too.

"Guys!" I call out to them but don't move. I've learned my lesson about racing off into the woods without a plan. On an impulse and a prayer. No, I'm staying right here. Dad would be proud.

"Over here! I found it." Sadie yells. A few seconds later, she pops her head through the bushes. "Oh you're gonna love this."

"What is it?"

"A Florida panther." She almost squeals in glee. Then her face drops and she appears serious. "But it's not good."

Dylan charges out of the bushes with blood on his t-shirt. He races to the car and leans inside the car to grab his walkie-talkie.

"Papa Bear, come in."

He waits for only a few seconds until Rex's voice comes over the static radio. ""Hallo, mooi een!" What's up Junior Bear?"

"You're not going to believe this, but we found an injured Florida Panther. About a half a mile up Mama Bear's road. We need help."

"Roger that. On my way," Rex says.

Within ten minutes, Birdee and Rex show up in Rex's truck and shine the lights into the woods.

Dylan leads Rex off into the trees with Sadie, and I follow closely on their heels. Birdee hobbles behind me due to her—as she puts it—grumpy knee.

I push back the weeds with one hand and peer in. Rex and Dylan are leaning over a bloody animal lying in the thick grass. When I see the Florida panther's face, I gasp and take a step back, covering my mouth. "Is it dead?"

The slender cat is about six feet long with four massive paws. Its eyes are circled by black trim and white around the mouth.

As soon as the animal hears me, it struggles against Rex's hold, scratching and snarling.

"Dylan, hold her down," Rex says.

Sadie steps out of the way while the guys work. "He's not dead...but badly hurt. Some jerk's probably put a trap out here."

"On my land! Better never get caught by me," Birdee hollers from the dirt road.

Rex shouts at her. "Honey, get my bag out of the trunk. I need my tools!"

Birdee stumbles off mumbling about someone trespassing on her property.

Rex grunts as the animal thrashes around. "Girl's strong, I'll give her that. Dylan, help me pin her down so she doesn't rip off her own paw."

Dylan takes off his t-shirt and wraps it over the cat's eyes. Then he practically sits on top of the panther while Rex inspects a large chain wrapped around the animal's paw. Caked blood tells me the cat has been bleeding a while.

I lean over them as they work. "Is it poachers?" I've grown up with them trapping animals and this isn't their trap of choice.

"Don't think so." Rex shakes his head. "They usually don't use chains. Someone's trapped this poor animal and kept her chained up."

He lifts up the edge of Dylan's shirt, exposing the animal's neck. A choke collar is embedded in the animal's neck. When Dylan touches it, the panther thrashes around obviously in pain, growling and snarling.

"It's okay, girl. I know that hurts." Rex takes his canteen and pours water over the animal's bloody, raw neck. "Poor thing."

Birdee comes up with the duffle bag. "Here you go."

Rex looks back. "Grace. Get me the bolt cutters."

I drop to my knees next to the panther and sift through the bag. The clanging sends the cat into another fit. I pull out the heavy tool Rex requested and hand it to him.

"Hold her head," he says. "And keep her calm. I'd like to go home with everything intact."

I sit next to the cat's large head while Sadie and Dylan hold the panther's paws down. The cat pants heavily, either from the awful heat or the stress. Maybe both. I stroke the soft space between her flattened ears, careful not to get close to her mouth in case she decides to snap. I don't know why, but I start to hum. My mom always does it to calm me down and it works every time. Who knows if it will work on a feline?

Sadie squats next to me. She takes out a bandana and pours her water on it. She studies the animal's neck, dabbing it with a wet cloth, and mutters under her breath. "Freakin' bastards."

"Do you know who it belongs to?" I ask.

She shakes her head. "Not definitely, but I can only assume it's from Uncle Bob's crap shack. It's only a few miles from here. Then again, there are tons like this. Chains and abuse all look the same." Her eyes water up quickly.

Before I can say anything comforting, she wipes her eyes and clicks a quick cell photo of the animal. She stands and walks off. "Dylan, can I borrow your truck?"

"Sure," he says without hesitation. "Wait. Where are you going?"

"First, I'm going to go to the media with this picture. Second, I'm going to plan another protest and get my dad involved. This is the last straw. And third, I'm going to make Uncle Bob wish he never met me." She storms off and a few minutes later, Dylan's truck putters down the dirty road.

Rex smirks at Dylan. "You got yourself a live one. That's for sure."

"The best kind." Dylan says, smiling.

"Think she'll be okay?" I ask.

Birdee laughs and pats my shoulder from behind. "Maybe you need to worry more about Uncle Bob and the mayor."

While I serenade the panther, Rex carefully cuts the chain off the animal's leg with his bolt cutters. Surprisingly, the animal doesn't move and appears calmer. She lies quietly with Dylan's t-shirt still masking her eyes.

"Well—" Rex stands and wipes his hands on his shirt. "That should do it."

In the dim light, I can tell he's serious. "What do you mean? What about the collar?"

"That is beyond my skills. Hopefully she'll heal okay." Rex says and stands. "But it's a nasty wound. Never know out here."

"Wait a minute." I shake my head but keep my voice calm. "We can't leave her out here. Especially not in this thing. She could die."

"You don't know that." Dylan says. He's still sitting on top of the cat, careful to keep his weight off the panther's ribs. "She might be fine."

I clench my jaw so hard, it throbs." How can you say that? One, she's tame; and two, she's hurt. We both know a wound can be fatal out here."

Birdee kneels next to me. Her knee cracks from the strain. "Chicken, we can't take this animal back to the house."

Rex places his hands on his hips. "She'll probably attack us as soon as she gets a chance. Probably hasn't eaten in days. Look at her ribs. This cat will put us on the 6 o'clock news as Dumb Locals of the Year."

"Wild animals are unpredictable," Dylan shifts a little so he can see my face. "Especially wounded ones."

"Duh," I say, thinking of my encounters with wolves and bears. I know about animals. Dad knew about animals. But like he always said, they are worth every risk, even if it only means we save one. "And so are people."

Rex laughs and pulls off his baseball cap to wipe the sweat. "She gotcha there."

"No," Birdee keeps her voice soft. "Dylan's right. It's too dangerous."

"But this cat belongs to someone. She's not so wild." I say it quietly as if I'm talking to myself. The animal's ears twitch as if it's listening to our entire conversation. "Maybe she's not so wild. Maybe she's tamer than we think."

"First, these animals never *belong* to someone." Birdee stands. I have to shade the rays of light so I can see her face. She doesn't appear happy, yet somehow, she seems unsure. "I mean, just because some nitwit trapped her and locked her up doesn't mean she was his pet. You know that."

The panther relaxes under my touch, but I continue stroking her head anyway.

"Birdee, we can't leave her," I say. "Even if she can walk, she'll surely get an infection out here the minute her foot touches that nasty swamp water. We have to at least take her back and bandage her leg. You have supplies at the house. You rescue animals all the time."

"Birds," she says. "Not wild, endangered carnivores."

"Same thing," I snap.

"Actually," Dylan pipes up. "They're very different animals. One is considered an 'ave' that eats worms and one eats meat...which means humans are on the menu."

"Shut up, Dylan. You're not helping things." I give him my evil eye and channel my inner Sadie. "Besides, if you jump in the water with a six-foot gator, you shouldn't be afraid of a cat."

He puffs up when I attack his ego. "I'm not afraid, just being factual."

"Birdee, please. We can't leave her out here..." I pause, wondering if I should say what I think I should say. It will hurt, but it will get my point across. I force out the words so

I don't change my mind. "Dad wouldn't. He'd never abandon a hurt animal. Never." I wait for her reaction, not sure if she's going to yell or cry.

Birdee remains silent, but her blue eyes moisten. I can tell she knows I'm right. She glances from me to the cat then back to me again. "Okay. But only for tonight. We'll have to call the ranger in the morning and get this animal to a real rehab center. I can't keep her long."

"Deal."

"Birdee?" Rex says slowly like he thinks she's crazy, but he knows he's treading on thin swamp water. "Are you sure?"

"You gettin' deaf, Rex? You heard me. We're taking the panther with us. No ifs, ands, or buts about it. Grace is right; Joe would have never left this animal behind. No matter what, he died for those bears, so if I die saving this panther, so be it!" By the end her voice is loud.

Rex nods at Dylan.

I mean how can he argue with that?

"Great." I smile at her bossiness. "So what do we do?"

"Dylan will have to hog tie her," Rex says slowly as if he's still not on board with the whole rescue plan. "Gently. We'll put her in the back of the truck."

"Wait. We're really doing this?" Dylan asks, eyes wide. "Taking home an endangered animal. Which is illegal by the way."

"I'll call Mike at the Center so he knows," Birdee says. "He'll take care of it in the morning."

Rex nods once and pats Birdee's hand. "No use arguing with two stubborn ladies. I've learned my lesson. If you can't beat them, join them so they don't beat you." He leaves for a few minutes and comes back with his boat rope.

Dylan carefully ties up the animal's paws while Birdee and Rex throw together a homemade stretcher with some tarp, sticks and rope. We keep the shirt over the panther's eyes to keep her calm and lift the animal onto the stretcher. She sags into the tarp without any movement. If her chest wasn't moving, I'd think she was dead.

I'm actually surprised the panther doesn't fight back. Maybe she's worse off than we think.

Each one of us grabs an end and walks out of the bushes.

"Jeez." My muscles strain under the heavy weight. "How much do these things weigh?"

"Since this is a female, probably about eighty pounds for a healthy full grown cat," Rex says. "Maybe lighter, considering you can see her ribs."

The four of us struggle to carry the panther to Rex's truck. My shoulders and arms throb and burn from the extra weight. I sit in the back with her as we creep down the road, careful not to hit any bumps.

When I finally see the lights of Birdee's house, I'm relieved. Rex parks and comes around to let down the tailgate.

"Where should we put her?" I ask.

Birdee assesses the area, deciding between the grass, the driveway, or her living room. "I guess you can bring her inside."

"You sure about this?" Rex asks, with a hint of concern.

"The animal hasn't moved the whole way; she's okay." When Birdee sees Rex staring at her, she finishes. "Just for now, until we get a plan."

Once we lay the panther down on the rug, I spread out a towel on the living room floor and get ready to bandage the leg properly. I watched Dad do it a million times, anytime a deer, bear, or even a rabbit had its foot caught in a poacher's trap. One deer was so bad off it lost his hind leg. There was nothing we could do. I remember the wolf I stumbled across last winter, lying deep in the snow. I tried to save him, but it was too late.

This is my chance to make up for that.

Petey flies in the room. "What in the wide, wide world of sports...?"

I stare at Birdee. "That thing must be a robot or something."

She smiles and shrugs. "What can I say? He's smart and *Blazing Saddles* is one of my favorite movies. Win-win." We both know it was Dad's favorite too.

"You're sick." I laugh as Birdee heads into the kitchen. Though I have to admit, she's right. That bird is smarter than half the people I meet. I whisper at Rex, "If she loves you *half* as much as she loves that silly bird..."

"...I'm a lucky man," He smiles and pats my shoulder.

"Yes. You are."

Birdee returns to the room with her bird rehabilitation supplies. She squats next to me and takes off her hat, telling me she's about to get real serious. We both roll up our sleeves and start working.

I hold the animal's head as she works.

Within a few minutes, Birdee has the animal's leg lubed up with medicine and wrapped in gauze. She and Dylan hold the panther down as Rex cuts the collar off her neck. It's embedded in some places but thankfully not as bad as it looked when we found her. I dress the neck wound. I try my best to wipe off the blood and pus from the infection. I bet I wince more than the cat does. I wonder if it's as painful as it looks.

Once the animal is bandaged up, Birdee reaches into her bag and pulls out a syringe.

"What's that?" I ask.

"Last year, Petey started plucking out his feathers. Guess he was stressed."

"Because birds have so much to worry about," I say.

Birdee gives me the eye. "Excuse me, but birds have feelings too."

"Only thing is, that's not a bird. It's a freak with wings. And there are only a couple things he should be scared of. A one-eyed stray cat getting glasses...or...me stuffing him."

"Chicken! You're awful. Don't you say that in front of him," she half laughs and half hollers, making the panther flinch. She jabs the syringe in a bottle and fills it. "Anyway, as I was saying before I was rudely but humorously interrupted, the doc gave me some anxiety meds back then to give him. Only I never used them."

Petey squawks and then shrieks, "Crazy as a loon."

I laugh, but keep my voice very low. "Ummm...maybe you should have."

"Maybe I will if he doesn't behave." Birdee gives Petey the eye and shushes him but addresses me. "Hold her head; I have to put it in her mouth."

"Seriously?" I ask. Because there's no way I'm sticking my hand in a panther's mouth. I've seen stories like this on the news and it never ends well. "You sure?"

"Hey, you started this. We gotta finish it," Birdee says as she squirts the medicine in the air.

"Move over. I'll hold her." Dylan bends over and pins the animal down with both hands. "If I can wrestle a 1,000 pound alligator, I can control a little ole kitty cat."

"That means I have to touch the mouth. Thanks," Rex says. He pries open the panther's mouth with both hands. The canines are at least two inches long. I hold my breath as Birdee squirts the medicine in the back of the panther's throat. If anything happens, this is my doing.

Fortunately, the panther doesn't respond at all.

Birdee sits back on her heels and exhales a long breath. "There. Don't say I never do anything for you. Just risked my life for a cat."

"Endangered cat." I remind her.

"Traitor!" Petey squawks and flies out the door.

"Better go after him," I say and then return to stroking her head. "Thank you. You're the best grandma." I lean over and kiss her on the cheek.

"And don't you forget it." She nods and uses the chair to push up.

"I won't," I say.

Rex whispers in my ear. "I'm guessing you are on permanent dish duty."

I smile up at him. "Now what do we do? How long until it takes effect?"

"Dinner is next." Birdee walks into the kitchen.

Rex follows her like a shadow. "I hope she doesn't mean we are on the menu."

"Chicken. Why don't you stay with the animal? She's sedated and will probably sleep through the night. I'll go make some dinner and bring you out some."

As the three of them leave, I sit on the rug next to the panther, watching her chest move up and down.

I reach over and slowly pull the t-shirt off her face.

And find two gold eyes.

At first, I scoot back a few feet. Afraid she may snap. But she doesn't move. Instead, she fixates on me.

And for a moment, we stare at each other.

Her bright yellow eyes—once eerie—now seem gentle and kind. Something about her expression convinces me that she isn't a threat to me. Or anyone for that matter.

The panther lets out a deep sigh as the medicine creeps through her veins. Her eyes close slightly and her body relaxes even more. Soon, her tongue juts out the side like a little kitten.

Now that the panther is asleep, she doesn't need to be bound in safety ropes. Reminds me of Aslan's death scene in Narnia.

"Easy girl." I slowly undo the knots at her ankles, careful not to touch her sore leg. When I'm done, I slide the rope away and scoot back.

The panther raises her head, which makes me flinch. If she wanted to, this panther could slice me in half with one swipe of her claws before Petey could say 'tweet. '

My heart pounds in my chest as she licks the gauze on her paw.

I remember the pretty Cherokee healing song Tommy used to sing Ama when she was in the hospital dying of cancer. The song used to make her smile. Though we never totally regained our friendship after everything that happened, I still think about him daily. If he were here, he'd sing the song. So I whisper the words under my breath in Cherokee and English. Not that the panther can understand either.

"Wani wachiyelo ate omakiyayo. Wani wachiyelo ate omakiyayo." The deep tones echo in the room. "Father, help me, I want to live. Father, help me, I want to live."

The panther stops licking and stares at me. Once again, her eyes remain on mine. Her pupils slip in and out of small slits as the light of the fire blazes behind me.

"Wani wachiyelo ate omakiyayo. Wani wachiyelo ate omakiyayo."

The majestic expression on this animal's beautiful face combined with the words I sing brings tears to my eyes. Not only do I miss Tommy, but the song makes me miss Dad all over again. It also reminds me of Simon, the little bear Dad and I rescued when I was younger. When Simon was still healing from his human encounter, Dad and I used to sit with him and sing this song together. Unfortunately, in the end, I couldn't heal Dad or Simon. Both were taken from me by poachers. People who didn't respect animals.

But here, now, maybe I can help heal this panther.

For them.

As I sing, I inch closer to the panther with my hand outstretched. Something in me knows she won't hurt me. Knows I am safe. I slip one leg under her head and wait cautiously. As I keep singing, she eventually lays her head in my lap.

I slowly stroke her head until she purrs.

Birdee walks in the room. She gasps and then hisses in a low voice. It's loud enough for me to know she's not happy, but quiet enough for the panther to stay asleep. "Grace Wells!"

I put my finger to my lips and point to the animal's closed eyes. "Shhhh. Never wake a sleeping carnivore."

She tiptoes over to me. "Is this a good idea?"

"Definitely not," I say in a low tone.

Birdee reaches over and pets the panther that is now sound asleep. "Your father used to say that too. Though it never gave me confidence before, and it still doesn't now. He always dragged home animals - anything he could get his hands on. Snakes, raccoons, even lizards with missing tails. I used to tease him that most of the swamp creatures lived in our house when we had a perfectly good nature reserve in our backyard." She draws her hand back slowly and shakes her head. "I didn't like that then. And I don't like this either. Not one bit."

I sigh. "Birdee, I know I don't always make the best choices. Even when I think them through. But that's me. I guess I listen to my heart more than my head."

Which is not what Dad taught me, but it's who I am. Who I've always been.

"Sometimes I have to go with my gut. It's not always right, but I really believe this animal is safe with us here. She won't hurt us."

Birdee leans against the couch. She doesn't talk for a while. The fire crackles and hisses behind us. Eventually, she strokes my hair and breaks the silence. "I will say...your father never brought home one of these gorgeous creatures."

I smile. Birdee always understands me. The way Dad did. The way I wish Mom could. "She is beautiful, isn't she?"

Birdee nods. "Do you know that panthers are great mothers? Raise their kittens all on their own. Without the father. They're loners and great hunters."

I feel guilty about not appreciating my mom more. She's had to do the same—raise me, feed me, take care of me even when she didn't want to—and she's doing the best she knows how. Considering her high school sweetheart was killed and her only daughter barely survived. My mom is one strong lady, and I don't give her enough credit.

I think of the panther's meaning. "Native Americans believed panthers were a symbol of ferocity and valor, protecting their loved ones. As a totem animal, they represent the dark side of the moon."

"How do you know so much Cherokee?" Birdee asks.

"Tommy," I say reluctantly because I know how she feels about him. "Native Americans called the Everglades *Pa-hay-okee.*"

She narrows her eyes. "Did Tommy tell you that too? You talk to him?" Birdee still hasn't quite gotten over the way Tommy lied. No matter his reason. All she sees is that his mistakes got Dad killed in the end. After she found out about Tommy's lies, she's never fully forgiven him. I don't think I have either. Though we both know deep down that Dad's death wasn't totally Tommy's fault.

It was Al's.

"No, I haven't." I shake my head and squeeze her hand. "Besides, Tommy only knows about fish."

"Well then, I can see why this creature likes you. You two are practically the same. Two wild, yet somewhat tame creatures stuck in a strange place." Birdee reaches out and strokes my hair. "Enough about all this. You hungry?"

I shake my head and sit back against the chair's cushion. "Nah. I'm going to sit here a while."

"Of course you are." Birdee stands and makes her way into the kitchen. She stops and turns to face me. "I almost forgot. I came out here to tell you something."

"What?" I wait for her to spill the beans. Her expression tells me the information is a doozy.

"Sweeney called." Birdee says. "They spotted Al."

I stop breathing for at least one second. "And?"

She looks away and mutters, "He's not in North Carolina anymore."

"Then where is he?"

She shakes her head but refuses to meet my eyes. "I don't know, Chicken."

My words stick in my throat. "What do you mean, you don't know?"

Before I can answer, the phone rings.

Birdee picks it up and after a few words, smiles weakly. She holds out the phone, "It's for you. It's Mo."

I can't stand quick enough. But I refrain from jumping up and scaring the panther. Instead, I gently lay its head on the towel and fast-walk into Birdee's office. "I'll get it in here."

My hand shakes as I pick up the phone. "Mo?"

"Hey blossom," He says softly. "How are you?"

"Hey!" Hearing his voice makes my heart sing. I can't hold back my smile. Though I don't let Mo catch on to any of this. Ever since Mom and I came down here to live with Birdee, our relationship has been strained from the distance and stress. And I'm not sure how to fix that, considering this move is semi-permanent. But I don't need to add to it by drilling him about it every time we talk. "Birdee says you found Al?"

He pauses for a second too long for my taste. It means he's unsure of his answer. "Yes."

"If he's not in North Carolina, where is he?"

Mo clears his throat but it doesn't wipe away his thick English accent. "He was spotted near Tallahassee."

"Tallahassee?" My throat dries and I grip the edge of the table to keep me from tilting. "So he's in Florida?" The thought of Al in the same state gives me the creeps.

He tries to make his voice sound upbeat but I can tell it's strained. "Don't worry. He doesn't know anything about you and Birdee. We've seen to that." Not only is Birdee's house in her mother's maiden name, but the FBI has performed tricks to eliminate any trace of me.

"O...kay. But what if he figures it out?" I say slowly, trying not to sound worried. I don't know what I'll do if Al shows up. The thought of seeing his face again makes me cringe.

"He won't," Mo says. "Trust me."

I swallow the lump in my throat. I do trust him. It's Al I don't trust.

Both of us go silent. Not much to talk about when a mad man is on the loose and 800 miles keep us apart. It's funny how distance changes a relationship so fast. Not because feelings change, but because you aren't there for the little moments anymore. You don't get time to share the random thoughts that spring through your mind at crazy times. There's pressure to deliver great and happy conversation each time you talk on the phone. But in my mind, most good relationships are built on a string of small moments, not a tapestry of big ones.

I decide to change the subject. Our relationship feels strained as it is. Maybe we need to lighten up some.

"So, how are you? Sweeney working you hard?"

Mo laughs a little but I still hear the tension. Like a chain on a butterfly. But then he says, "Abso-bloodly-lutely", and I can tell he's smiling.

Then I hear him suck in a breath. My heart sinks. He's

probably as uncomfortable and as sad and as frustrated as I am. Knowing that the thing keeping us apart isn't going away any time soon. And until it does, Sweeney wants us to stay away from each other so there's no chance Al can find me. At least not before they find him first.

I'm not 100% convinced he won't. My luck hasn't been too great this last year.

"I miss you," Mo blurts out.

And there it is.

As always, Mo is the first to crack through the wall that I've spend so much time building and repairing and patching.

I clear my throat as tears prick my eyes. "Me too."

He waits as if to let my response sink in. "I mean...*a lot.*"

I smile and wipe one lone tear that has snuck out of hiding. "Ditto."

I want to say more but I don't know what to say. *I'm lost without you. Will we ever be together again? Do you still love me? Will I ever be safe again?* Instead, I remain still. Quiet. Guarded. Afraid. That's what my life as turned into since meeting Al last fall. Since losing my dad and Seth. Since moving here.

A whole mess of fear.

"Are you okay?" he asks.

I force myself to connect, to say anything that will mean something. "I'd feel much better if I had a strong, young, handsome agent by my side. Probably safer too."

"I'm not an agent yet."

"If you keep working this hard, it's only a matter of time."

This backfires and makes Mo exhale in frustration. "Not sure I want to anymore. It keeps me away from you."

This melts my heart so I step out a little and throw a life-line. "I love you, Mo."

"I love you too, Blossom. I wish so much I could come and visit. But Sweeney doesn't want me anywhere near you.

And I don't blame him. So far, I haven't exactly made your life easy. In fact, some may think I've made it worse."

My voice shakes as I force out words. "No. Don't say that. You've made it better." He has no idea!

"Not sure anyone else agrees with you. Not Birdee. Not Sweeney..." He pauses. "Not even me."

The words slice through my heart like a knife through flesh. They hit me hard and force me to fall back in the chair. I check over my shoulder to see if Birdee's listening. Or worse, Petey.

I play off what he said and try to lighten the mood. "Man, you are so drama. I'm fine, and I'm better with you. How about if you sneak away and drive 800 miles for a kiss?"

This time he laughs hard. "On your bike."

"Nah, a bike would take too long." I smile at Mo's silly English phrase, which means absolutely nothing in translation. A poor alternative to America's popular F off. "A car might be much faster."

"You're a silly billy, Grace Wells." Mo says. I can hear the smile in his voice. My spirits lift again. I can still make him happy, so maybe there's hope for us yet. "And I love you for it."

"I hope there's more than that."

"So much more," he whispers. "Look. This will all end soon. Then I promise I'll take some time and come down. We can go fishing."

"You mean, I can fish; you can try." A flashback of when I first met him pops in my head. He was a bait fisherman—the total opposite of my flyfishing—but he was cute. Some things I can overlook.

"Very funny." His voice sounds a bit hurt but maybe he's playing. That's the thing with the phone or email—you can't tell, so it makes you paranoid. I bet most of the time when my feelings are hurt by something he writes or says, it could have been solved with a face-to-face conversation instead. Still, I can't help but want to assure him about us. Maybe it will assure me too.

"I love fishing with you, among other things," I say. "Or we could go alligator wrestling. Dylan's been teaching me."

"Don't let him *teach* you too much," Mo grumbles. "Or I'll have to come down and help him learn a hard lesson."

"Oh brother." I giggle at his overprotectiveness. "So that's what it's going to take to get you down here? Anyway, he has a girlfriend."

"What's she like?"

I decide against mentioning my attendance at the protest with Uncle Bob. No need to worry Mo more than he already is. "She saves animals and he twists alligators in figure 4s so I guess they're perfect for each other."

"So are we, Grace." Mo covers the phone but I can still hear murmuring in the background. "Crumbs, I gotta go. Sweeney's calling me. He'll kill me if he knows I'm talking to you. Even if it is from a payphone."

"They still have those?" My words are light, but they feel heavy on my tongue. I know Sweeney's only protecting me—like he has been for months now—but he's starting to get on my nerves. Going days or weeks without talking to Mo is wearing me down. "We'll talk soon, right?"

"I hope so. I'll try. You just be safe. Lay low and don't do anything...impulsive."

"Me? Never." I sit up straight and wish I could think of something important to say so he stays on the phone. Something profound. Something that leaves us feeling good about each other. But I got nothing. "If you hear of—"

"—If I hear of *anything*, I promise, I'll let you know. Bye Grace." Then he simply hangs up.

"Bye," I whisper to dead air and poke the OFF button, severing the only connection Mo and I have right now. All the things I wish I'd told him stream through my head. Why I didn't tell him about the alligator Dylan attacked? Or the panther we saved? Maybe if we talked about something other than Al and the case, it would do us some good.

My dad always said, *what you focus on gets bigger.*

And he's right.

Petey squawks from the corner, "I love you." Then he makes kissing noises.

I throw a pencil at him and lower my voice so Birdee doesn't hear me. "Someday, you'll make a nice pillow, Petey."

He squawks, "Mayday, mayday."

Birdee races into the room rubbing a dishtowel between her hands. "Good night, what's all the racket?"

"Your loud bird. What else?"

Petey flies over my head and lands on her shoulder. She gives him a sunflower seed and eyes me.

I avoid the stare and leave the room. I bend over and crawl up to the panther, still sleeping, and lie next to her.

Birdee follows me with her hands on her hips. Her bright blue eyes are thin slits, telling me she's assessing me and my actions. "What happened?"

I shrug, playing down my feelings. Sometimes I get tired of talking about them. Tired of me. "Nothing. I just miss Mom and Mo. Hate being sequestered down here. Away from them."

Birdee sits on the chair. "Is that how you feel? Sequestered?" Voices from the T.V. hum in the background, but I don't listen.

The hurt in Birdee's eyes is obvious. She doesn't deserve my ungrateful attitude. "You know what I mean. I love being with you. Here. But I miss Mo. I miss Mom. I want to go home. To my home. I know we'd all be together if it wasn't for the mess I've made over the last year."

She reaches over and strokes my hair. "I fail to see how

this *mess* is all your fault. Katie was bat-shit crazy and Al's the wackadoo. As far as I'm concerned, you're the only who's done anything worth a damn. The only one's who's done the right thing. Selfless things. You've sacrificed more than anyone...and I'm sorry you're scared."

I glance up at her. "I didn't say I was *scared.*"

"You didn't have to, Chicken."

To avoid showing her what's really going on inside, I bury my head in the panther's yellow fur. Birdee's right. I am scared. All the time. Day or night. I try to pretend like I'm not because it all seems too unreal. Too crazy. People stalking teens doesn't happen to small-town people like me. Or does it? It always feels so farfetched when I watch a news story on the T.V.—a missing kid or a tragic accident—but somehow, that craziness is now happening to me. Only I can't turn the channel.

That familiar lump expands in my throat. No use crying. Tears never wash away anything anyway. All they do is make things more real and make you feel weak. Conquered. Vulnerable.

Right now, I need to be strong. Or at least try and act it. Dad always said *we gotta fake it 'til we make it.*

I'm just getting tired of faking.

"You think this will ever be over?" I gently stroke the panther's head. "That Al will ever get locked up for good?"

"I hope so." Birdee hugs me from behind. "For all of our sakes, but especially for you."

I rub circles along my forehead. "Why is this happening to me? What did I do wrong?"

"Nothing. But there's no use feeling all sorry for yourself. Moping about. It doesn't help you or anyone. Nothing's happening now anyway, except maybe dinner. Food will cheer you up."

Pretty sure meatballs and green beans aren't the key to happiness. "I'm not hungry."

"Not even for this?" Birdee holds out a Mint Chocolate MoonPie.

I sit up and smile. "Oh, well...I'd *never* turn down one of those."

"Didn't think so." She hands it to me. "Don't worry, Chicken. Everything will work out."

I open the package and take a bite of my favorite treat. "I want to live my life without always looking over my shoulder."

"For now, you'll have to live and focus forward. You're safe here."

She glances over and the TV and grabs the remote. "What's this?"

I catch the leftover new story from Sadie's protest and cringe when I see myself walk up next to her. Almost don't recognize myself. My hair looks longer.

Birdee listens to the protest and the commenters talking about Sadie's young age. "That girl is ballsy. I'll say that. Don't care how young she is, she has done more in a month for this world than any of the bozos in suits."

Then it cuts to a couple pictures, of a boy and girl. She holds the remote close to her eyes until she finds the volume button and makes the TV louder.

"This is another reported teen runaway that has gone missing. First there was Joey Miller. He left his parents' home and lived on the streets for a while before disappearing. Then there was Parker Neill who broke out of rehab and was never seen again. Now, Annie Christopher, a well-known local runaway, is nowhere to be found. More on this story at eleven."

"Good lord. What is going on with this world these days? I can't even watch the news anymore. It's either too depressing or too scary." Birdee tosses the remote on the table and heads into the kitchen.

Once she's out of sight, I glance out the window at the dark swamps that lie beyond her borders. An owl hoots in the distance and the crickets chirp. I think about everything she said. I'm sure she's right. Yet something in my gut tells me that things may not work out the way she wants them too.

Sometimes things get messy before they get clean.

In the wild, stress and fear may cause you to make bad or impulsive decisions.

When I open my eyes the next morning, I'm surrounded by yellow fur, infused with the smell of the swamps.

It takes me only a second to jerk up into a sitting position. I rub my eyes. When I notice the panther sleeping, I smile.

I, Grace Wells, slept next to an endangered Florida panther.

All night long.

I almost want to cheer. I mean, who gets to have spend-the-night parties with animals? Let alone these gorgeous creatures. The perk of being part of a nature lovin'—and dwelling—family.

I stroke the panther's head. Dad would totally freak out if he knew I was this close to a wild Florida panther. That I've spent almost twelve hours with one. In the house. As far as he was concerned, the closer the encounter, the better. Within the proper safety parameters.

Though I'm not 100% positive this measures up to those.

The panther slowly opens her eyes as if her lids are heavy weights, probably still groggy from the medicine. She stretches her front legs. Daggers pop out the ends of her paws and scrape across Birdee's favorite rug.

I move to my feet fast and hop onto the couch, putting a safe enough distance between us. Just in case she's not as thrilled with her bedmate as I am. From a distance, I check out her wounds while she's not paying attention.

They're no longer goopy, but they still look disgusting. As I watch her lick her damaged paw, I can't help but wonder what crappy zoo she came from. Maybe Uncle Bob's, though it's still a couple miles from here. If it's not his place, that means another zoo is hiding somewhere along the Everglades border.

The panther sits with a regal look on her face and stares at me as I flip on the T.V.

Birdee scuffles in the room, wearing her robe and slippers. The straw hat is perched on her head, ready for the morning chores of feeding rescued birds in her homemade aviary. Come to think of it, the woman always has that hat on. Probably sleeps in it and dreams of all the Peteys she will help the next day.

"Here kitty, kitty!" Petey squawks from his perch.

The panther flinches and lays her ears back on her head. She hisses once and pushes to her feet. The large cat is much bigger than I previously thought. She paces in a circle. Even though her paw is injured, she isn't limping too badly.

I stay on the couch, a safe distance away. "Oh! You want to eat *Petey*? Is that it?"

When Petey hears my threat, he flies toward the kitchen and says, "Nothing to see but feather and bones."

I roll my eyes. That bird is too much.

The panther moves toward me.

Instinctively, I scootch back in the seat until the couch practically swallows me.

She hobbles closer until she's sitting right in front of me.

She sits and rests her head on the edge of the couch like my dad's dog, Bear, used to do. She gives me the same pathetic look Bear did when he was hungry. He would sit for hours and stare at me, waiting to be fed.

I reach out and touch the soft bridge of fur between the panther's eyes. Her face relaxes and within seconds, she purrs loudly. Only it sounds more like the sputtering motor of a broken down car.

"You're a big softie, huh?" I say, rubbing her nose. "Not a mean bone in your skinny little body. We need to pack you with some food...great, now I sound like Birdee."

I slowly stand as to not shock the poor animal and inch toward the kitchen. The panther limps behind me and watches as I search through the fridge. I toss last night's leftover steak and some bacon onto a plate. Surely Rex won't mind sharing his leftovers.

And what he won't know won't hurt him.

The panther sniffs the air and perks her ears.

I rest the plate on the ground and back away a few feet. I do not want to come between this cat and her food.

The panther limps over to the plate and smells the food a few times.

"Beggars can't be choosers, cat. Eat up."

As if she understands me, she laps down the food.

"Hallo, mooi een!" Rex walks in the kitchen and stops when he sees his sirloin gobbled up in one big bite. "So much for steak and eggs for breakfast."

"Sorry, guests get to eat first. Even furry ones."

"Guess I'll settle for some bacon then."

"Oops," I point to the dish. "She ate that too."

He smiles and grabs his baseball hat off the rack in the corner, pulling it on his baldish tan head. "Guess I'll have to starve for the well-being of an endangered species."

"The world thanks you." I glance past him. "Birdee's outside with the birds."

"That woman never sleeps. She's always doing something. Chickens and birds are already fed. They eat before we do." He thumbs over his shoulder. "She's in her office talking to the wildlife guy. They're coming out this afternoon to pick up...the cat."

"Panther...and she has a name."

"Really?" He pours some of the old coffee from yesterday and heats it up in the microwave. "Dare I ask?"

"Sylvester." I say, trying not to smirk. I've never been that creative with animal names. My dog was Bear, and my bear was Simon.

"As in Tweety Bird?" Rex asks as he slurps a sip of steaming coffee.

I smile. "No other."

He dumps in several packets of sugar as if it's a replacement for water. He watches the panther licking the empty plate. "Isn't this beauty a girl?"

"Hmm, good point. I forgot that part. Guess that means Garfield and Felix are out too?"

He slurps the coffee from the alligator shaped mug. "You watch cartoons? Figured they weren't cool anymore."

I shrug. "Guess I'll stick to Cat."

"Ahhh, a throwback to the old days, Audrey Hepburn in *Breakfast at Tiffany's*. I like it. Classic and minimalistic." Rex grabs his bag and heads toward the door, patting my shoulder as he passes by. "Evidently, I gotta bring home more bacon. Take care of *Cat*."

I smile and call after him, "Then you better get lots o' bacon!"

As he walks out, Petey performs a fly-by that is way too close to the panther's head.

The panther perks up and growls, swatting the air with

her huge paw and clipping the tip of Petey's tail. A gray feather floats to the ground. Instead of flying away like a normal bird afraid of its historical enemy, Petey performs a quick U-turn and attacks.

Cat hisses and yowls, ducking as he skims by her head one more time.

"Petey! Stop! Go away!" I try to shoo him off, but the panther is now between him and me, and she's still growling.

The panther turns her head for a split-second, giving Petey enough time to peck her on the head like a warplane dropping bombs. Then he coasts back up to his safe perch.

The panther is startled and races toward the door before I can blink.

Petey squawks as the panther runs by. "Petey won."

The panther crashes through the screen as if her leg and neck were never injured and sprints outside.

By the time I reach the door, I watch her leap into the tall grass and disappear into the Everglades.

"Cat!" I run after her. "Cat!"

Rex is standing by his truck. He calls after me. "Grace. Wait up."

I stop at the edge of the yard and breathe heavy while he catches up to me.

"Where do you think you're going?"

"After Cat," I breathe out each word.

He frowns. "In your bare feet? Not exactly the choice of hiking footwear for these parts."

"Oh," is all I can say.

Birdee hobbles up to us. "Good Lordy me. What's all the hoop-la-la? Can hear you all carrying on inside."

I keep my eyes on the thick border. "Cat's gone. Petey attacked her."

"Stupid bird!" She curses her pet, now sitting on a branch high above us, and throws her fist at the air.

"I should stuff my pillow with your feathers!" She yells at the sky.

"What should I do?" I say, panting. "She won't make it out there alone."

Rex grabs my shoulders. "She seemed fine to me. Don't worry so much. That panther knows this place better than all of us put together." He walks to his truck, already running, and climbs in. "Don't do anything stupid."

"He's right, Chicken."

I shake my head. "No Birdee, he's not. I saw her limping this morning. The adrenaline probably took over after she freaked out. I have to go after her."

"Just wait. Let me go call the wildlife place back and see if they can send someone out right now." Birdee walks me back to the door with her arm around my shoulders. "I'll be right back. Maybe they can help us find her. Plus Dylan's on his way, too. He and Sadie wanted you to hang out with them today. They're coming here any second. Okay?"

I nod. "I guess. Okay."

Birdee heads back inside to make her call while I stand outside, staring at the tall grass blowing back and forth.

A loud growl sounds off in the distance and then all goes quiet. I'd know the sound of that horrible screeching anywhere. A panther's call is not something you forget after you hear it once. The tone of it is like no other.

I race back inside and grab the phone to call Dylan but he doesn't answer. I slam down the phone. "Shoot!"

Cat is close. If I hurry, maybe I can catch up to her. With her leg, she can't have gone too far. I pace a little and bite my nail. That itchy impulsive feeling—that's been missing for months—slowly returns. I have to find her. I don't know why, but I just do. Maybe I'm afraid she'll run to Bob's place.

Instead of racing off on a whim, I take a deep breath and think it through. I jot down a note saying where I'm going and quickly mark a small map, informing Birdee of my tracking plan. That way, Dylan can come after me as soon as he gets here. He and Sadie will find me quicker than anyone.

I grab my hiking boots and backpack complete with the necessary supplies and my knife. Like a fireman, a hiker's pack is always ready to go at a moment's notice. I shove a walkie-talkie in the bottom as a safety precaution. Not many cell phone towers in the Glades.

Before Birdee can return to stop me, I dart out the back door, jog across the yard, and slip into the tall grass.

Sometimes I don't always do the best thing. I know that.

But I try to do what I believe is the right thing in the moment. Which is not always very popular or void of any risks.

I check my watch coordinates to stay on point. This time, I've got everything I need to be safe. What's the worst thing that could happen? I'm convinced Cat is not dangerous, so my only danger is maybe getting a little lost. But not for long because Dylan is coming. Only my ego will take a direct hit, because Dylan will tease me forever.

My goal is to make sure I find Cat before Bob does.

And find her before it gets dark.

The Everglades isn't the best place to hang out. Especially after the lights goes out.

I 've learned one thing about myself over the last year.

I'm impulsive.

Dad always said stubbornness was my biggest enemy in the wild. I never thought he was wrong. I'm trying to work on it, but when my heart clutches onto something tight enough, all logic drains from my brain.

I rest on a dead cypress tree and check my coordinates.

It's been a couple hours now and still no Cat.

Not sure if she's scared or hurt. It's possible I'm tracking the wrong animal.

I bend down and run my hand over the sand until I spot another paw print. It's definitely some kind of cat. Whether it's *my cat* or not is the question.

I take a drink of water from my canteen and secure my pack. Then I pull on my baseball hat to block the sun and follow the tracks farther down the thin path.

In the distance, a panther shrieks, but I can't tell from which direction.

Instead of turning back, I veer deeper and deeper into the Glades.

Since Birdee lives on the edge of the national park, it is easy to hike in any time—away from the noise, away from swamp tours, and away from all the tourists. The Everglades is the most remote area in the South, a sure way to be alone.

The sludgy path is sprinkled with puffs of bright green ferns and different colors of orchids—purple, yellow, and white. When I was little I thought the Glades was filled with only swamps and water. But I quickly learned there is a little bit of everything out here—swamps, forests, and plains. Whenever I miss my home in North Carolina, I hike into the hammocks where oaks, cypress trees, and willows stand along the edge of the deep swamps. The thick, lush trees—though very different from the Smokies—make me feel right at home.

The only difference is the sticky humidity.

I pour water onto my bandana and wrap it around my neck like a boy scout. If the swamps don't kill you out here first, the unbearable heat is a dead second.

I hear another cat call and veer right, keeping my eye on the prints. They appear to grow larger. Then again, sometimes tracks spread in the soft mud.

Up ahead, I spot a few scratches along a tree trunk. I check the grooves. Definitely from some kind of large cat. Bear feet are wider and their claw marks run deeper.

Through the trees, a flash of yellow breaks through the green and brown backdrop.

Cat.

Picking up the pace, I follow the tracks. They lead to the edge of the woods that borders an open space. A large roar rides the wind.

I stop at the tree line. The little hairs on my neck prickle.

I don't know my cat calls very well but that didn't sound like a panther to me. It was much deeper. Louder. Florida panthers have high pitches and long wails. More of a screech and a hiss mixed together.

I squat at the edge of the clearing and peer through the thick brush. Across the grassy field, I make out the outline of a run-down home. I pull out my binoculars and search the property, scanning the fence line until I spot a sign.

Uncle Bob's Animal Park.

I pull back from the viewer. Crap. Somehow, I've hiked a few miles and come up on the back of his property. I shift my position closer and scan along the house. On one side, a bunch of cages are stacked on top of each other. My stomach sinks. During the protests, I couldn't see any of these from the road.

No wonder Sadie's pissed off at this guy. Her obsession with Uncle Bob makes much more sense. From the road, I couldn't see all this. Now, the same fire ignites in me. I sit there watching the animals in total disbelief. How can something like this happen here? There's a freaking fake zoo barely a few miles from my house, sitting on the edge of the Everglades—home to several protected parks. Reminds me of the bear pits sitting on the Indian reservation in my hometown.

The two don't belong together.

As soon as my eyes focus in on the first cage, my heart cracks. A ghastly-thin tiger cub lies in one corner of a pen. For the few minutes I watch him, he doesn't move. As time passes, I become worried that he's dead. Anger and panic urge me out of hiding. I want to run, scoop up this poor animal, and take him someplace safe. I want to save him. But trespassing is a local and federal offense. The tiger cub is bordered by a huge grizzly bear on one side and a pen of gray wolves on the other.

It's like I'm back in those woods. Searching for Dad. Finding those cages. All the abused and starving bears milked for their bile. Bears paws cut off fresh kills and packaged for shipping. All for money.

Suffering pays.

I decide that there are worse things than trespassing. Like indifference.

I watch the property for a few minutes longer. When I get to one cage, I stop.

Cat sits in the corner, licking her paw. The thick, heavy chain is looped around her neck again.

Anger forces my fists to ball. She must be in pain by now because the medicine's probably worn off. I can't rescue all these animals, but I definitely won't leave Cat here. Whether I'm trespassing or not.

When I'm sure no one is around, I race across the field. I make my way along the side of the house and sneak up behind Cat's cage. As I move closer, the smell punches my nose. The zoo's perfume is a strange concoction of rotting food, crap, and urine.

Next to Cat, a house of screeching monkeys notices me and goes ape shit.

Cat's ears twitch at the noise but she continues licking her leg.

I slink along the perimeter. Past bears, past wolves, and past all the other abused animals. I wait behind Cat's cage, checking the area before I put my plan in action. If the owner is close by, he won't appreciate me creeping around his property. The dude was aggressive with Sadie and she wasn't even on his land. The shotgun. The yelling. The threats. I can only imagine what he'd do if I got caught on his property. Pretty sure Uncle Bob won't play around.

Once I think it's safe, I creep up behind the panther's cage. "Cat. You okay?"

The panther whips her head in my direction and stands. With her hurt foot drawn up, she limps over to the fence on three legs and rubs her head along the side of the chain links. For being so abused and neglected, she sure is friendly.

I poke two fingers through the fence and scratch her head. "You poor thing…" When I notice the chain digging into her blood-red neck again, tears spring to my eyes. When will we, as humans, ever learn to treat animals the right way? With even an ounce of respect. Many of us do it right, but there are too many of us that don't give a crap.

I pull on the cage to test its strength. "Don't worry, I'll get you out of here." I move around and jiggle the heavy padlock. "They've got you good."

The panther follows me around the pen as I search for a way in. I head to the rear of the pen and check all the latches. One is rusted. I pull out my knife and try prying it apart. It's tight, but it loosens, giving me hope I can bust this cat out of here. And fast.

As I'm digging at the hinge, something roars and slams against the cage behind me.

I jump forward, dropping my knife. It clatters on Cat's cage floor.

I quickly grab it and turn around just as a huge male lion throws himself against the cage behind me, trying to swipe his hand through the gate. He studies me with hunger and rage.

I almost have a heart attack until I realize he can't bust out.

He continues to slam against the wire barrier. Over and over. His side is smeared with blood, probably from the jagged fence cutting into his skin.

I try to calm him down with my voice. "Easy, boy. Easy."

The lion bares his huge fangs and roars. His eyes lock onto mine. I try to glance away but at the same time I'm fascinated by his utter handsomeness. Even though he appears ultra thin, he's still as fierce as any animal I've ever seen.

He snarls, displaying his fangs, and stalks me as I frantically work on the latch. When he roars again, Cat races over, ignoring her hurt foot, and snarls a nasty panther growl. The kind that makes you want to cover your ears.

I step in between their cages and get her attention. "It's okay. He can't hurt me."

I keep jimmying the cage as Cat paces behind me, following the lion back and forth like a mirror image.

The panther is protecting me, which I find totally amazing. Here is an animal that's supposed to live out her life in the wild, having cubs and lounging in a cypress tree. Instead, she's illegally captured and stuffed into a 12x12 prison. Even though she's hung around me for less than a day, somehow, she still wants to protect me.

This makes me want to jailbreak her out faster.

I pick up my knife and keep the lion in my peripheral vision as I work. The whole time praying the cage is strong enough to prevent an attack. I chip and dig and pry until the hinge releases its grip. I wrap the bottom of my t-shirt around my hand and bend back the chicken wire to create enough space for Cat to squeeze out.

Somewhere around the side, a vehicle with a loud muffler drives up. The engine cuts off and footsteps crunch along the gravel. A man hums, triggering my biggest fear. Al.

I yank the wire doors back together. Cat stops on the other side, confused. I squat down and motion for her to stop. Like she can speak sign language or something. She sits and watches me intently, as if waiting for the "go" signal. Sometimes, I forget how smart animals are.

We all do.

My heart pounds. If I'm caught, not only will I get hit with trespassing charges, but there's no way of knowing what this person might do. Especially if he figures out I'm stealing an endangered cat that probably brings in a crap load of cash.

Never eat the bread and butter of someone starving.

People who live off the grid don't follow society's rules. Nor do they want to.

The man mutters on the phone. Something about a white alligator and $50,000. Another under-the-table deal.

The footsteps grow closer. Luckily, I'm hiding behind the cage. Unless the owner walks back here or stares in my direction, I'm hidden.

The man approaches the lion's den and picks up a metal pipe. He trails it down the cage, creating a loud noise.

The animal charges and slams into the fence. Growling. Slashing.

The man doesn't flinch. He's not the least bit scared. Instead, he continues harassing the poor lion. Teasing and goading it into a frenzy. "Come get me, yah big hairball! I need me a new fluffy rug." The noise launches the lion into a state of insanity. The racket sets the monkey house up in arms. The ruckus must upset Cat because she starts pacing, even with a bad leg. Limping back and forth. Back and forth.

The man obviously gets bored quickly and moves on, approaching Cat's cage. I press my body to the ground that smells of urine and mud. I pray he doesn't see the hole in the cage. Or me.

He rattles the cage with both hands. "You're lucky I have a heart, cat. You escape again; next time I'll shoot you dead on the spot. I need the space. Got more animals coming in that'll make me some big cash. So watch yourself. You hear me?" He kicks the fence hard.

Cat flattens her ears against her head as she growls and hisses.

The man cackles and moves on to terrorize the family of monkeys.

I remain hidden until he's out of sight and exhale the hovering fear. If I could release all these animals, I would. Hopefully, they'd hunt down and feed on this moronic morsel of a man. Chances are they're not all as tame as Cat and probably have been food-deprived for months.

A hungry tame animal is more dangerous than a wild well-fed animal.

Once I'm sure the man is gone, I stand and open the cage. "Come on, Cat. Let's get out of this dump."

The panther watches me. Her ears rise back up to a perky position. She slinks toward me with her head down in a cowering stance. I coax her to safety and slip the rope through the collar. Her neck is still bleeding from the chains, but she still lets me touch her.

When I lead her out, I hear someone walk up behind me.

I freeze, afraid to turn around.

"What the hell do you think you're doing?"

When I spin around, Dylan is standing there. His hands on his hips and a scowl on his face.

"Jesus, Dylan!" I press my hand against my chest to keep my heart from bursting out of my body. "Scared the crap out of me."

"What the hell are you doing here, Grace?" He keeps his voice low, but his gritted teeth and strained tone tells me he's yelling on the inside.

"Rescuing Cat." I hold up the rope. "Petey scared her off and she ran here."

"So you decided to come alone and do your B&E for the week?"

I shrug, not knowing what to say. Other than, "I wasn't going to leave her."

A higher voice pipes up. "You did the right thing."

Dylan shakes his head and even stomps his food slightly, like a child begging for a sugar fix in a candy store. "Sadie! Don't encourage her."

Sadie walks out from behind the monkey pen. "She's definitely got balls." Sadie beams when she sees me holding the rope. "Grace, I must say, you sure don't disappoint."

I'm not sure what else to say besides, "Thanks."

Sadie bends over and strokes the panther's head. "Hey beautiful." Cat purrs at Sadie's touch and rubs against her hand.

"Named her yet?" Sadie asks as she strokes Cat's ears.

"Cat," I say. It's not until I utter it out loud that I realize how dumb the name sounds.

Sadie raises her eyebrows. "Original."

"Our bird named him." I say, before realizing how stupid that sounds too. This pretty and poised girl—dressed like she walked out of an REI commercial— simply stares. She's obviously super smart. I, on the other hand, sound like a total buffoon.

"So your talking bird named him Cat? Awesome!" She slaps my back and almost makes me choke on my pride. "Man, I like this girl."

"Yeah?" Dylan smirks, obviously still peeved. "She's smarter than she looks."

"Gee thanks. How'd you know I was here?"

Behind me, Sadie has jumped into action, taking pictures of the animals in their pens. The whole time she captures the horrors, she talks. "This is freakin' great. Wait 'til the eleven o'clock news gets these photos. They're going to shit a story." She moves around the cluster of cages, frowning at the conditions.

"Dylan, will you help me get Cat home? Before Bob gets back."

"Home?" Dylan crosses his arms, but keeps his voice low. "Newsflash. Birdee's house is not this animal's home, nor is it a licensed sanctuary from this nut job."

Sadie obviously overhears. She beelines over and frowns at Dylan. "You're right, the Everglades are."

My heart hides in my stomach when I realize Sadie's not in my corner.

"But…. that isn't exactly feasible, is it Dylan? Where else would Grace take her?" She throws a wink in my direction.

He shoves his hands in his cargo shorts pockets. "Come on, Sadie. Give me a break. This is illegal. We take this animal to Birdee, to Rex, we open ourselves up to a swamp of trouble."

"How can you say that?" Sadie's voice moves up an octave, like she's sucked in a hit of helium. "Are you suggesting we leave this panther here?"

Standing behind Sadie, I throw Dylan a 'told you so' look. It's nice to have someone on my side for once. Someone impulsive. Someone crazy. Someone who welcomes trouble way more than me.

Dylan sighs. He doesn't even put up a fair fight. Instead, he submits to his master. "Fine. Let's get this cat out of here. Now."

"Wish we could take them all." I can't help but watch the animals—now they are all looking back at us through their cages. They're probably wondering if we're rescuing them too. Saving them from this life of abuse.

"Nope. Not an option." Dylan says. "We'll take the panther but that's it, or we'll be inviting trouble to a party we don't wanna throw."

"This sucks." Sadie's disappointment spreads across her face that's been wiped clean of her resolve. She shuffles down the row of cages, kicking up puffs of dust. At each pen, she stops and speaks sweetly to each animal. I can't hear her but I can only assume she's apologizing for her pending abandonment. At a time when they need her persistence most.

Sadie whispers to the lion that tries to swipe off her head. She laughs with a hyena. And she monkeys around with the lemurs. Yet no matter how much they rage or chatter, the girl never finches, she never retreats…not even once.

I like this girl. A lot.

When she done making her rounds, Sadie returns. "Okay, let's go. Bob is coming back soon and trust me, we want to be long gone." She moves to the end of the cages and peeks around the yard before motioning us forward. "Come on."

Dylan and I stand next to Sadie. I can't tell if I'm scared or excited. My heart bounces around in my chest like a bouncing ball as Sadie whispers a countdown. "1…2…3…go!"

I suck in a deep breath and race across the lawn. Dylan and Sadie are right behind me.

Even with the limp, Cat doesn't leave my side, like a heeling dog. Fascinating thing about an animal: it never expects anything in life to be fair and square, never complains about pain, and never carries a grudge. They do what they have to do.

When we reach the tree line, a deep voice surfs the heat waves. "Hey! You kids! Come back!"

I glance back quick enough to catch sight of Bob running with a shotgun. For an old man, he sure is faster than I expected. Or hoped.

Sadie yells to us, "Spread out!" She veers to the right. Dylan runs straight. I turn left, heading away from the zoo. But into the Glades. The panther zigzags alongside me as I weave through the palm trees and crash along an overgrown path.

A gunshot rings through the swamp.

Cat jerks against the rope wrapped around my wrist.

The jerk is shooting at us! My heart gears up into over-drive and the adrenaline pushes me to run faster. This mission just shifted from an animal rescue into a crazy chase. I figured Bob was mad, maybe even unstable, but I didn't count on him wielding weapons.

I race along the soggy ground. Sliding. Skating. My feet splash through mud and water and sludge.

Once my heart is sure to explode, I drag Cat into thick bush webbed with roots to rest. My chest heaves as I gasp for oxygen, taking in very little air. Feels like the door to my lungs has been slammed shut. Nothing in or out.

Tromping noises tell me someone is close, too close. I slip the rope off of Cat's head. If things go bad, I don't want the makeshift leash to get tangled up and hold her back from freedom.

Footsteps and heavy breathing follow. Getting closer. Closer.

I hold my breath and bury my face in Cat's neck to hide any sounds that may slip from my mouth. I can't help but wonder if Dylan and Sadie are okay. If Bob is here with me, hopefully they got away. I sit with Cat for several minutes until finally, the steps fade.

When I'm sure it's safe, I crawl out of my hiding place. The sky has darkened in the short time we've been in the swamps. Being in the Everglades at night is never a good plan. I check my compass and head back in the direction of home. Cat follows closely even though she is leash-free.

When I cut around a corner, something hard slams down on the back of my head.

Cat skitters off at the noise.

I try to move past the pain, but the blow knocks me off balance. I hit the ground, landing on my shoulder. Pain sprays through my body.

As my vision fades, I hear a voice say, "Gotcha!"

SURVIVAL SKILL #10

Panic is more dangerous than almost anything. It interferes with the operation of your best survival tool: your mind.

I open my eyes. I have no clue where I am.

Eventually, my vision adjusts to the room's dim lighting.

I'm in a rustic cabin somewhere. Dingy. Dusty. Empty. Old sheets hang over the windows. The smell of mold is strong. I scan the deserted space, void of any furniture. I spot my backpack in the far corner.

I close my eyes and try to remember what happened. As my brain unfogs, thoughts piece together. *Running with Cat. Hiding from Uncle Bob. Feeling pain.*

As it all gushes back, my body tightens. My stomach cramps and my mind races.

This guy's gonna to kill me. I know it. A sea of panic rises to high tide. Ideas swirl inside my head but I can't seem to focus on one that will help me get out of here.

Oh God. I need to escape this dump before Crazy Bob returns.

I try to stand and, for the first time, realize my hands and feet are bound. I struggle against the plastic ties binding my hands and ankles.

"Help!" I yell and stop to listen for any reply. Silence. "Hello? Is anyone there?" When no one answers, deep down, part of me is relieved. If I'm flying solo, then that means Sadie and Dylan got away. Then a sick feeling floods my gut. But if they aren't here, then that means I'm trapped. Out here. Alone.

A faint noise drifts through the thin wall. I slither to the corner and press my ear against the wood paneling. Listening. Hoping. I pound my hands against the wall a couple times and close my eyes. Waiting. Praying.

Then a muffled knock.

I sigh and press my forehead against the wall. Thank God. Someone else is here. But who?

I push myself onto my knees and force myself to stand. Once I balance myself, I hop to the window and part the makeshift drapes with my clasped hands. As far as I can see, rows of pine trees wade knee-deep in a sea of saw palmettos and spiky shrubs.

No doubt about it. I'm deep in the Glades. One of the most remote places in the nation.

Great.

I jiggle the doorknob. Locked.

I lean against the wall and study the zip ties. This guy doesn't know a thing about tying people up properly. The #1 rule of any good kidnapping: always bind the hands in the back. Duh.

A long time ago, Carl showed Wyn and me how to break free of any binding: zip ties, duct tape, even rope. And though Carl ended up the bad guy and, ultimately, responsible for Dad's death, he was close to my family for many years.

A surrogate uncle to me. A stand-in father to Wyn. A trusted friend to Dad.

All lies. All gone.

I move past the fear stirring inside—don't even want to think about why I am here or what he will do. I close my eyes, focusing on everything Carl taught me in the weekly defense class. I imagine the technique and prepare. Wrists in. Tighten zip ties with teeth, pulling so my hands turn pale white. Stomach tight.

I pray this works. I methodically go through each step.

I stand against the wall and tuck my elbows close to my sides. I need enough force to pop these suckers open. I can do this. I've done it before.

I can do it again.

I close my eyes and exhale. Focus. Breathe. I raise my clasped fingers above my head. This better work. I don't have time for do-overs.

"1...2...3." Arms up. Swing down. Slam wrists against gut.

The force pops off the ties and they drop to the floor.

"Yes!" I rub my wrists until the blood and feeling returns. I use one of the ties to jimmy the lock, releasing my feet. Once I'm free, the adrenaline takes over. A surge of newfound energy bubbles to the surface, drenched in hope.

Now for an escape plan. There's one window and the door is locked. I remember my backpack. This guy's obviously an amateur. The #1 rule of any solid kidnapping: ditch the belongings. Deep breath. In. Out. In. Out. I can't let my nerves take over. It causes carelessness. Most important thing in any survivor situation is not to panic. I grab Tommy's knife from the bag, throw on my backpack, and squat in front of the door, listening. Thinking. Planning.

I can battle the hinge, the window, or the doorknob.

Using the tip of the blade, I remove the tiny screws around the rusted plate until the doorknob falls in my hand. I jam the end of the knife in the hole and click the lock open.

I smile. Almost free.

I yank the door.

Bob's gun greets my face on the other side. "Hello." He sneers like he spouted off a dirty joke. "Going somewhere?"

I reverse, gripping my knife behind me back. If I charge this guy, he'll overpower me. With my size and weight, I won't stand a chance against a crazy old man with a gun. I slide the knife into the back of my pants and wait for my surprise attack later.

Bob invades the room and shuts the door to my freedom. Only a sliver of light peeks through the doorknob's hole. He glances down at the floor and picks up the broken zip ties. He rolls it between his fingers. "Very clever, Grace. You're gonna be a great catch. I like that."

Catch? No clue what that means. Yet fear invades my senses. A taste of metal covers my tongue. My heart beats in triple time in my ears. And my limbs get numb and tingly. I straighten my posture and throw out my chin, hoping to show nothing but pure confidence. Hoping to mask my weaknesses. Hoping to fake my strength. Hoping to buy some time until I can uncover his plan.

"Why am I here?"

He takes one step forward. "You were trespassing."

I retreat. "So …you *kidnap* me?"

"You and your little friends were snooping around on my property." He shrugs, like kidnapping a teen is no big thing. "Not my fault. Took the law into my own hands. Keep it private. Only way to go nowadays. I don't need any more trouble."

"Not sure kidnapping qualifies there." My throat grows scratchy, like I've swallowed a shot of gritty sand. "Are my friends here?"

Uncle Bob charges forward, making me cower in the corner. He cups my shoulder and forces me to the ground. "Shut up. Don't want to hear any more."

"What are you going to do?"

Uncle Bob moves close to me. "Nothing...*yet.*"

I squint to try and make out his facial expression in the dark. I'm confused. "Nothing? Why did you bring me here?"

He shrugs. "To scare you. Teach you a lesson."

Funny. I don't see this guy as the teacher-type. "Sooo, you're going to let me go?" My brain twists in a knot. Not sure which thought to unwind first. I'm confused. Why bring me here to let me go?

Bob removes a tin of tobacco and stuffs a clump into his cheek. The smell reminds me of Dad's partner, Les with his tobacco stuffing habit. Never thought I'd ever miss Les. Until he saved my life, I thought he was guilty of poaching. Of hurting my dad. Of being a traitor. I wasn't a big fan.

Now, I consider him a friend.

I take a step toward the door. "So then you're saying I can leave."

"Sure," When I move, he steps in front of me, blocking my path. "But not right now."

My stomach spin-cycles out of control and my hands turn slick. I try to breathe in the Incredible Shrinking Room. But the images of being trapped in the cave with Mo, harassed by Al, and betrayed by Carl—they all flood my head. I place my hand against the wall to steady myself. I dig deep, trying to tune into to my inner badass. But I'm worn down.

Tired of being lost. Tired of being strong. Tired of being scared.

"I...I don't understand."

He spits in a cup. Les used to do that. Only Les isn't here to rescue me this time. No one knows where I am. Not Birdee. Not Rex. Not Mo.

This time, I'm totally on my own.

Tears press against the back of my eyes.

Uncle Bob smiles—as much as a lion can smile if a lamb shows up for dinnertime. "Your name is Grace, right?"

My eyes float up and meet his. "How did you know that?"

"They mentioned it on the news."

"What news?"

"Your little escapade with that Sadie chick went statewide. All over the main channels. Anyone who was someone in Florida probably saw it. Department of Agriculture called me after. For an inspection on my place."

Me? On T.V.? I didn't think about the cameras. Or that the story would air so quickly. Or live for that matter. No clue it would travel out of the small town of Everglade City.

I wonder who else saw it.

My eyes slide to the door. Before I can make a run for it, Bob backs toward the door, grinning from ear to ear. "Don't get too excited. I have a surprise for you—so you don't get too lonely."

"Hmm, can't wait." My nerves zing out of control. "Some food I hope. Taco Bell would be nice."

Uncle Bob unclips his walkie-talkie from his belt. "Bring them in."

A few minutes later, the door opens. One man pushes Sadie inside, followed by two men clasping Dylan's biceps, both of which are bigger than the girth of their legs combined. Both have blindfolds over their eyes and their hands are bound behind their backs.

Sadie yells from underneath the cloth, struggling against her captor. "Asshat! Get the hell off me."

The man pushes Sadie and she stumbles to the floor. She uses her legs to push back into a standing position, which is hard when your hands are bound. She talks to the opposite wall, not knowing where anyone is standing. "I never stay down. Don't you forget that."

The other two men drag in Dylan. They appear much smaller compared to him and his large build. For some reason Dylan isn't putting up much of a fight. Like the Hulk being held down by a hare. They throw Dylan down on his knees and quickly leave.

I get it. If you punch a bear, you better run before it can punch back.

Uncle Bob hovers in the doorway. "I'll be back."

"Can't wait!" Sadie hollers after him, her voice as sharp as my knife.

Bob doesn't respond. He just laughs and slams the door.

"I knew that bastard was bad, but who knew he was cray-cray?"

I peek through the doorknob hole. A couple men walk away from the cabin to a clump of tents. They all lay down their guns and sit by the fire. However, both of Dylan's handlers stand outside, guarding the entrance. I count six men.

"He's gone but his mutts are still here." I try to remove Sadie's blindfold but she jerks away and kicks my shin.

I grip both her arms. "Sadie, stop...it's me." She stops resisting on cue. "Grace? Oh shit Dylan, he has Grace too."

Dylan stays on his knees. "I thought so."

I pull off Sadie's blindfold and can tell she's been crying. Black streaks trail down her cheeks. "We were hoping you got away."

"Ditto." I shrug and we hug. "You okay?"

She nods and then pulls Dylan's blindfold down around his neck so he can see. She hugs him and kisses his face all over like she's so happy to see him. "As much as I love your kisses, I'd love to feel my arms again."

"Oh—sorry, baby!" She sets his wrists free and then hugs him again. "I thought they hurt you."

Dylan laughs as he rubs feeling back into his arms. "They wish. I've seen alligators that shit bigger than them."

While Dylan and Sadie continue their reunion and whisper how worried they were about each other, I move to the window and peek out again. "What do you think is going on?"

Sadie massages her wrists—still blood red from the tight ties. "I don't know. But whatever it is, it isn't good."

I lick my lips, cracked from the dryness and thirst. "You think he's going to kill us?"

Dylan walks next to me. "He's crazy but he's hopefully not totally insane. A killer. He probably wants to scare us into leaving him alone."

Something doesn't sit right with me. I press my hand against my stomach to ease the upset. "I don't know. I have a bad feeling."

"I'm sorry guys. I got you into all this." Sadie's voice cracks like an old record. "I shouldn't have asked Dylan to come to the protest."

I spin around and face her. "You didn't do this. You've been protesting his place for months. I'm the one who went to Uncle Bob's after Cat and started snooping around. If it wasn't for me, we'd all be eating patties and pies at Birdee's place."

"Blaming someone isn't going to help any of us." Dylan runs his big hands through his long blonde hair. His muscles twitch as if they are preparing for battle. "Let's focus on getting out of this place before he gets back."

Sadie springs to attention. Like someone pulled her string, forcing her to liven up and talk. "We could make a run for it."

"Wait!" I hold my hand out to her chest. "There's a guy right outside the door. You'll never get past him."

"They'll shoot us before we reach the trees. Nowhere to hide out there. Like a freckle on a baby's butt." Dylan says the last line without laughing so I know he's equally stressed. "We have no idea where we are. No supplies. No water. We'll have to wait."

"For what?" I ask, searching for some idea of a concrete escape plan. I need to know I'm getting out of this dump. Right now, my flip-out switch hangs on a tiny wire. "He said he'd let us go. Right?"

Sadie gives me a look like I'm stupid; yet, with her hair and eyes, she's more likely to be the crazy one. "Yeah, sure, and I like fur coats."

"We need to come up with a plan. This will be much harder than you think."

"I say we go for it. I'd rather run for it than end up a beached whale." Sadie paces the dirty floor, kicking dust up into the air. My eyes burn and my nose itches. "I overheard them talking about some hunting game when they thought I was out of it still."

"A game? Like a joke?" My brain still refuses to believe this guy is on a kill mission. But the more information I get on this guy, the more I sweat. I yank the t-shirt away from my body, praying the extra sliver of space will allow me to breathe better.

"Doubtful." Sadie says.

"I heard it too. Couldn't make out all of it but sounds like they like to hunt animals." Dylan says. "Some kind of ongoing challenge."

I sit in the corner and hug my knees. The more these two talk, the more I want to throw up. "Wait...these guys *hunt* in the Glades?"

"Of course they do!" Sadie hits her fists against her legs. "That's the whole freakin' problem with these zoo asshats. They don't care about animals. Hunting to them is like eating to us. Not only that, they don't respect animals so they buy them illegally too. Problem is catching them in the act is practically impossible."

My brain thump thumps from the information. It's happening all over again. Someone is out to get animals, I get in the way, and then all hell breaks loose. "Maybe we can stop these guys. If they're talking about hunting tonight, we should wait. Sneak out after them and get proof so when they let us go."

The faint knocking sound returns.

"There's that noise again."

Dylan pushes his hair behind one ear, pulling back the veil so he can hear. "What is it?"

I crawl over to the earlier spot and press my ear to the damp wood. "You guys hear that?"

Sadie and Dylan do the same. We all look kinda stupid staring in a line with our heads pressed against the wall.

I close my eyes to concentrate. A few seconds go by and nothing. Then I hear it again.

Tap, tap, tap.

"Someone's on the other side of us." I strain to hear, wishing I knew Morse code. "Someone must be in trouble."

Sadie doesn't miss a beat, nor does she sugarcoat anything sour. "You mean besides us?"

I'm not exactly sure how long we sit in the hot, dusty room with our ears to the wall, trying to communicate. At one point, I smack myself a couple times to wake up. The rush of adrenaline combined with shutting down and settling down in the unbearable heat makes me sleepy.

I can't help but notice the sun has already gone down. Only a gray sliver streaking through the sky, reminding us that there once was a sun. And darkness is not permanent. The sun always rises. It's a matter of when.

A voice approaches the hut. I pinch Dylan and whisper to Sadie, "Wake up." She looks up at me with groggy eyes that would make a Bassett Hound jealous. I point to the door. "Someone's coming.

The three of us stand and wait for the door to open.

One of the men from earlier walks in. "Grab your things and follow me." And that's all he says. Nothing cordial about it. But nothing deadly either. Just Switzerland-neutral.

Sadie puts her hands on her hips and stands her ground. "And why should we?"

"It's time for you to leave."

We all exchange looks, surprised at his request. Maybe this Bob guy will let us go after all. Maybe he only wanted to scare us. Get Sadie to stop picketing his business.

I snatch my backpack. Either this guy is too dumb to notice or too smart to care. The three of us follow the guy outside. As soon as we pass under a light, I notice this guy has changed out of the white bully t-shirt and the ragged jeans. He's now sporting army fatigues.

"What's the occasion?" I ask from the rear.

He ignores me but Sadie practically growls like a hungry lion and chows down on the bait. "You're going hunting, aren't you?" She mouths, *told you.*

The man keeps walking so I can't see his face. "You could say that."

I holler out again. " It's illegal to poach animals in a National Park."

He nods and faces forward. "Ain't never been caught yet."

"Well that's about to change dirtwad." Sadie scoffs and hits him in the back once. "I'll see to that."

The guy stops and faces her. "Don't touch me again. Or I'll make sure you are first to go."

Dylan grabs Sadie's hand and pulls her closer to him, away from the camo guy. He keeps his voice low but I still hear what he says. "Chill out. We're not out of here yet."

"I will not." Sadie frowns and jerks away. But she quickly gathers herself and grabs his hand as if to apologize.

The man leads us to a group of men sitting in a circle, cradling rifles on their laps like babies.

We three sit on a log in the middle and wait and wait and wait. The waiting has my guts spewing around in circles, making me want to hurl. I cover my mouth just in case.

I search around. Besides the run-down cabin (that now resembles a few man-made shacks) and the tent city they've created, there isn't anything else around for miles.

"Where's Bob?" I ask.

The man who retrieved us stuffs his pocket with ammo. "He's coming."

"And he's letting us go?"

The other men smile as the head guy answers again. "Yes."

Another man speaks up. "What else would we do?"

The group laughs, making me shift on the log. Something doesn't sit right with me. I grip the straps of my bag for security. If they take my backpack, I'm going to lose it. I focus on the night sounds, letting them calm my nerves. I repeat mantras in my head.

Everything is going to be okay. Everything is going to be okay.

As I relish the peacefulness of the night sounds, something crashes through the woods.

I glance over my shoulder and scan the sparse trees behind us. The noise grows louder. And louder.

"Must be Bob." Dylan whispers and pats Sadie's knee. "We're almost out of here. Stay calm."

"I'm fine. He's the one you should worry about." Sadie balls her fists and then releases as if doing strengthening exercises on one of the squeezie balls. "But don't think, for a second, that I'm not gonna to take a cheap shot at this guy the minute I get my chance."

Dylan kisses her forehead. "God. I love your spunk. Especially the odds are stacked against us."

The crashing sounds continue like elephants are marching through piles of parched sticks. I study the men to make sure they're not listening. "Seems too loud for a man. He weighs under 200 pounds."

"Maybe he's got more men with him," Dylan whispers.

I study the group more this time as the noise continues behind me. The men don't seem fazed by the noise, which in some odd way calms me. If it was a bear or a panther, they'd be on their feet, fully armed. Most of these men are probably older than Dad. But one boy stands out. He's standing in the back, almost hidden from view. He can't be much older than me.

As I watch the men cleaning their guns or sharpening their knives, I think back to that day in the woods when I found the poaching campsite. Over a dozen men mutilating bears, milking them for bile. A few, including Carl and Chief Reed from the reserve, counted the money. I'll never forget when Mo pulled off his hood. I could not believe he was involved in something so horrific. At the time, I had no idea what to believe, even after he told me he was trying to pay back the guys who killed his father. And who ultimately also killed mine. What sticks out to me now was how my body felt that moment when I first saw him. All the feeling left my body and I felt my heart break in two pieces. Even after he explained, something shattered in me that day.

Something I can never get back.

The same feeling I have now.

Uncle Bob appears out of the woods with a large shape lumbering next to him. "Ah good. Our guests are packed and ready to go."

It takes me a second to realize his furry sidekick is the huge liger we saw at the protest. The massive animal lumbers toward us. What a beast. His head is as large as a grizzly bear's and his back reaches my chest.

We all stare at the strange hybrid, afraid to move, as it moves closer.

"Sit." Bob takes a whip off his belt and whips the animal. Even after the abuse, the huge animal stands still, as if deciding whether he will accept the command, and then plops his butt on the ground. Even sitting, he's taller than me.

Uncle Bob pats his pet's head with one hand and holds the chain with another. "Meet Hercules. He's a beaut, isn't he?"

The three of us don't utter a word. We can't. Personally, I've never seen an animal so enormous except for pictures of the Saber Tooth Tiger.

"Course, not all ligers are this big. Hercules weighs over 1,000 pounds. Eats over 100 lbs. of meat a day. How do you think I get that kind of food out here? Gotta hunt something."

Sadie doesn't speak. Instead of a smart, tough comment, she takes one step back. Her eyes wide. Her hands clenched.

It's the first time I've seen her retreat and the only time I have seen worry in Dylan's eyes.

Their reaction sends my fear spiraling like a roller coaster. Crashing down into my stomach and then slowly climbing up my throat.

Uncle Bob nods to one of his men. The man disappears into another shack and reappears a few minutes later. He's dragging someone behind him. The person fights back, mumbling from under a black pillowcase. Her feet are dirty but the red toenail polish gives her gender away. The man drags the poor girl to the front by Uncle Bob and yanks off her hood.

A young girl has duct tape over her mouth and wrapped around her hands like silver cuffs. Wide-eyed and groaning in fear, she looks around in a complete panic. Mud smears down her cheeks and across her forehead like war paint.

"Ho-ly shit," Sadie mutters out of the side of her mouth. "It's that missing girl they've been hunting for."

That's when I recognize the dirty, tattered girl. It's the runaway from the news. The one that vanished over a week ago. She's dressed in the same clothes as the picture on Nancy Grace. Tattered black pants. Dirty white t-shirt. She's alive and has been here the whole time.

Uncle Bob strokes her hair. "It's okay. Don't be afraid."

The girl muffles a scream and jerks away. When he grabs her by the hair, she struggles against his grip, trying to kick him. She's definitely a fighter. Won't go down easily. I already like her.

Sadie whispers in my ear. "Bet she was the one we heard knocking on the wall. Wish we had tried harder to reach her."

The girl—I think her name is Annie—and I lock eyes. I try to give her a 'you-will-be okay' smile, but honestly, I can't lie to her face. Right now, I can only hope he lets us go together.

And if he does, I'll take care of her. Because I know how it feels to be ripped away from your family—everything you know—and shoved in a hole. Held against your will.

Unfortunately, I know it all too well.

Uncle Bob nods at the man who lets go of her and shoves her toward us. The girl stumbles toward us. I step forward and catch her in my arms before she falls to the ground. I help her up and keep my arms around her. She feels frail and she's shaking like a caffeine addict who's snorted coffee. She smells of sweat and mud, doused in fear.

I rub her shoulder and smooth her matted hair. "I got yah. You're going to be all right. Okay Annie?"

She appears surprised I say her name but she nods very fast. Wanting to believe what I say. But the smear of panic and fear that fills her eyes breaks my heart.

I recognize that look.

She thinks she's going to die.

I start to remove the piece of tape covering her mouth.

Uncle Bob picks up his rifle and clicks his tongue. "Wouldn't do that if I were you. She's a god damn screamer." A few men cock their guns. The sound is louder than anything I have ever heard.

I drop my hand. "Please let us go. We'll take her with us and we won't say anything. To anyone."

"That is the plan." Uncle Bob faces the line of men like he's about to give them a war speech. "You boys ready?"

They all cheer and hoot, firing a few rounds into the air.

The girl next to me quivers uncontrollably. Like she's freezing. Only it's 95 degrees out here. At least.

Dylan removes his shirt and wraps it over her shoulders. His muscles bulge in the moonlight but he doesn't care. After knowing him only a few weeks, I know the girl is the first thing on his mind. Dylan always thinks of himself last, putting everyone else first. He glares at Uncle Bob and steps forward. "Stop playing games and let us go."

"When we're ready," Uncle Bob says.

"Ready for what?" Sadie asks.

The leader laughs and the other men chuckle behind him.

"Junior! Come up here." Uncle Bob waves over the young kid hiding in the back. "Time to become a man, son."

The boy shuffles forward with his hands stuffed in his pockets like he's searching for change. No expression except for a quivering lip. He approaches Uncle Bob and then turns to face us. Hunched over, head down, slumped in uncertainty. His body language tells me he's uncomfortable with whatever is about to happen. Like he knows something. His eyes scan upward and he tries real hard to scowl, to look mean and scary.

I bet he's about to pee in his pants.

I keep my arm around the girl who's now got her face buried in my shoulder. Soft whimpers find my ear as she cries under the strip of tape.

Sadie finds her voice. "Can we get on with this? I'm bored."

"Oh sure." Uncle Bob tosses his rifle to the boy. "You ready to hunt?"

"Yes." The boy mutters the word but it sounds more like a question than a statement.

Uncle Bob eyes Annie. "You ready too?"

Before I can blink, the runaway girl jerks out of my arms and bolts across the field. The tape on her hands prevents her from running fast enough. Her bare feet cause her to stumble as she trips over rocks and twigs.

Uncle Bob rolls his eyes. "Dammit all!" He hollers at the pensive boy. "Well? Go get her!"

It takes me a second to realize what exactly he's

commanding the boy to do. When the boy raises the rifle, I start to run after her but Dylan grabs me with both arms in a bear hold, holding me back. Keeping me safe.

He growls in my ear. "Don't."

The frantic girl runs and stumbles through the thick weeds. Every few steps she peers back at us. Her path is erratic like she doesn't know which way to go. Which way is safer. Which way is home.

The boy draws up the rifle and aims for Annie. His arms are shaking, either from the heavy load or the fear of harming another human being. He squints into the sight and hooks his finger on the trigger.

"No! No!" I scream out, too loud, and my throat instantly turns raw. I jerk against Dylan's arms. "What are you doing? Let me go. Sadie, do something."

Sadie stands next to me with her hand clamped over her mouth. Saying nothing. But she looks like she's about to haul-ass out of here.

Dylan hisses at her to stay back.

We all stand there. Helpless. Guilty. Conflicted.

I finally scream. "Annie. Run!" because there's nothing else to say or do. But watch.

Uncle Bob waits for a couple more seconds as Annie moves further and further away. His impatience peaks and he storms over to where the boy stands. Finger still on the trigger.

Uncle Bob snatches the rifle from him and throws the boy to the ground. "Get out of my way." He raises the rifle.

I only squeeze out one word when the gun explodes. "No!"

I watch in horror as the girl goes down.

For a second, the world slows down. Her hands fly up and her body thrusts forward before she disappears in the tall grass.

"Oh my God." I bend over and put my hands on my knees. The trees spin in a circle. An acidic taste rises in my throat. I try to swallow, but my body won't let me do any normal function. It's shutting down. My legs give way and I crumple to the ground. That poor girl was gunned down like a wild animal.

And I did nothing.

I bury my face in my hands and try to hold back sobs.

Sadie mutters, "Jesus Christ," followed by Dylan's long sigh.

For once, he's speechless.

Uncle Bob hands one guy his gun and pats his liger on the back, "Dinner is served, Hercules. Go." He lets go of the leash and Hercules bounds off to claim his meal.

My breath jerks in and out as my lungs convulse. I can't breathe as panic and reality all settle in together for the night.

Uncle Bob isn't letting us go home at all.

He's using as a prey.

For his biggest hunt yet.

In the wilderness, there are many predatory animals. Stay alert.

Dylan, Sadie and I huddle together. Frozen. Shocked. Scared.

If Annie got gunned down and mauled…we're next.

Uncle Bob walks up to the boy and slaps him across the face. "Boy, don't you ever hesitate again or you'll find yourself running."

A man from the crowd steps forward, "Bob, don't."

Uncle Bob faces him, "Don't? Your boy almost cost me a fresh hunt. Phil, if he wimps out again, I'll kill him myself. We can't let people rat us out."

Phil joins his son and pulls him out of sight.

Uncle Bob's words echo in my head. He's telling the truth. He is going to let us go.

He's not going to let us live.

My throat is dry and swollen. I want to cry but I'm stuck. Even in this heat, my body is frozen to the earth.

Uncle Bob faces us. "Well, that wasn't much of a hunt, was it kids? Little filly got ahead of herself."

"You're sick. Sicker than I ever imagined." Sadie glares at him like she wants to hunt him down and gut him herself.

Her eyes water with a glimpse of tears that she refuses to let see the light of day. She mutters, but loud enough for us to hear, "I'm so taking you out."

He ignores her buzz and speaks with his men a few minutes, making sure his back is to us so we can't hear.

I nudge Dylan who's been awfully quiet. "Do something?"

"Like what?

"If you can take on an alligator." I keep whispering out of the side of my mouth. "Surely, you can take on a few men."

Dylan leans down. "Alligators only hunt for food. These crazies hunt for fun.

"Whatever happens, we'll have to run in different directions." I clear my throat and keep an eye on Uncle Bob and his posse. "That way they'll have to split up. We have a better chance of taking them on if they aren't together."

"No way—we should stay together." Dylan shakes his head. "Power is in numbers."

Sadie watches the men to see if they're noticing our football huddle yet. "Dylan, she's right. If we run in different directions, it will separate these dingdongs. But if we stay together - they can all shoot in the same direction. Odds are - they'll hit one of us."

"Sadie…I don't want to…"

"Hope you're not worried about me because I'll be fine." Sadie grins and lightly pecks his cheek. "I'll even race you home, baby."

I don't say anything because I'm not sure how she can sound so light and confident. "The only way home is to divide and conquer. Trust me." The line scrolls through my head as I second-guess myself, praying I'm right. Dad would say the same. We won't stand a chance against these guys as a group.

Uncle Bob walks up with his men flanking him. "Party's over, kids. Time to deal with the devil. Here's the game. The three of you are going to run and we're going to hunt you down. No dirty tricks."

"Ha!" Sadie says in his face. She even has the overconfident head roll. "Over my dead body, Bobby."

"Well good. Cuz that's the idea." He leans on his rifle acting all casual. Like we are on a fun paint ball mission. "We will give you a one hour head start before we hunt you down."

"That's big of you." Dylan says.

Uncle Tom reaches into a cooler sitting off to one side. He pulls out a few waters and tosses one to each of us. "Don't say I'm not nice. Sure don't want you slowing down due to the heat. Dehydration doesn't make for a very fun challenge."

I stare at the water bottle sweating in my hand. "You're insane."

"Why thank you." Uncle Bob bows like he's on a stage show. "Should have thought twice about causing my property problems. You wouldn't have been on my radar. We usually like the less conspicuous."

"Big word, Bob," Sadie says.

He paces in front of us. "There are no rules. Anything goes. We will hunt you down fair and square. None of that technology crap. If you make it out, you get to live. If not, well then you know the ending."

"What makes you think we wouldn't tell anyone if we got out?" I shake my head as I say it. This is all surreal. A man hunting kids on a nature reserve? Reality is much stranger than fiction.

"I wouldn't know." Uncle Bob faces us and pulls on his chin. "No one has ever done that. Meaning we have caught every one. Every time."

"There's a first for everything."

Sadie checks out Dylan and me. A wily smile cuts through

her face and she narrows her eyes. "Is this a joke? This must be a joke. Right?"

"Don't make jokes. I'm dead serious." Uncle Bob picks up his rifle. He pulls out a box of ammo and loads his weapon. The men behind him take his cue. "One thing. You only get the hour if you make it away from this spot without being shot first. Ready?'

How do you say yes to that?

"On your mark."

I jolt to attention and quickly gather myself. I'm not sure which way to go, where to run, or what to do. I glance over at Sadie. She gives me thumbs up like this is a potato sack race. She doesn't appear the least bit scared. Just focused.

"Get set."

She points to Dylan and then east. She motions for me to go north while I assume she's heading west.

I nod, still unsure of the plan. But there's no more time to think it through.

"Go!" A gun shot goes off close to me, making my ears ring.

I take off straight, veer right, and never look back.

I run faster than ever. Faster than the time I found the camp in North Carolina. And faster than the time last winter when I thought Al was chasing me.

I pump my arms and jump over small bushes. I need to get to over the plain and into the trees without getting shot. Only then do I have a chance.

A gunshot sounds off behind me. I belly flop on the dirt, not knowing which way the bullet went.

A scream fills the air. I can't tell if it was Sadie or Dylan. Or if the men are hooting in glee.

I pray that Sadie and Dylan are okay. I'm not so concerned about Dylan. He grew up on an African reserve and has been living here long enough to know the lay of the land and how to survive. Experienced many animal encounters. It's Sadie I'm worried about. How much experience can a mayor's daughter have in the swamps? I'm thinking, not so much.

I hope they make it. Because no matter what Sadie says or what Dylan thinks, they're here because of me. And, I can't be responsible for another death. Not directly or indirectly.

My heart can't take it again.

Another gunshot explodes.

I lie on my stomach in the tall grass for a few seconds longer. Even though my chest is pressed to the ground, I gulp in enough air to slow down my breath. Once it is silent again, I push up to all fours and crawl through the grass on my hands and knees. Safer than running.

For now.

When I reach a single pine tree, I scramble behind it. About fifty more yards, beyond the field, and the thick woods will shroud me. The hammocks. That's where the real race will begin. Not only are strange men chasing me on a bizarre hunt, but there are a crap load of other challenges I'm going to face. Alligators, dangerous plants, murky swamp water, venomous snakes, deadly bacteria—you name it, it's out there. This is not a race to the finish.

It's a race to survive.

I crouch over and head toward the woods. Quietly. One step at a time. I separate some grass and get ready to head through the open field. When I peek through the opening, I freeze.

Hercules is straight off to my right. His back faces me and he stands over Annie's body. All I can see are her legs. Trails of blood mix with dirt and swirl along the ground. I cover my mouth with the back of my hand to keep back a gag.

My heart wants me to check, see if she's still alive. But my head knows better. I missed my chance to help her. And now she's dead. I want to run in her direction but I stop myself.

Pretty sure Hercules won't let me get close.

At this point, I can only hope he stays preoccupied. Then I can slip across the field and into the woods without any confrontation.

I test the wind. Lucky for me, its direction blows in my favor.

I take in a deep breath and inch out into the open. Taking one step in front of the other. The liger doesn't know I'm here yet. He's too focused on his meal. I pick up the pace, keeping my eyes on Hercules at all times.

His ears flinch and he sniffs the air. I'm not sure if he heard me or saw me, but I don't wait to find out. I take off running so fast, I practically stumble my way across the large open space. The tree line moves closer and closer, urging me to safety. As soon as I break the leafy barrier, I stop.

I am home. This is where I'm the most comfortable.

I take in the area for a split second and dash off down a sparse path, around bushes, and through mud. No matter what, I don't stop. I need to make up some ground before the night consumes the light. The dark is safest part of the day for animals. But the most dangerous for humans. Especially out here.

Luckily, I'm still in the dry part of the Everglades. Once I hit the swamps, my race home will take much longer, so I need to make up ground now.

Part of me wants to turn around—go back and find Sadie and Dylan—but there's no telling which direction where they are or where they are headed. They're probably not even together. I have no choice but point east like we planned and keep going until I get find some place safe. As I move deeper inside the forest, the already dim light continues to fade.

Luckily it's summer and the days are longer, giving me more light.

Eventually I stop to rest. I haven't heard any noise for a couple of miles. I sit down and pour a few drops of water onto my bandana. Then I wrap it around my neck. The water chills the base of my neck, making me arch. I sigh in relief as my body temp comes down. A person can live much longer without food than water, so I have to stay hydrated and alert or I risk being careless. I check my compass, making sure I'm on the right trail.

Crack.

The loud noise grabs my attention.

I scan the bushes and spot something moving.

A low rumbling noise warns me. The liger comes bursting out of the vegetation like a bull. His massive head remains steady as he bounds after me. He pads through the vegetation with a grace, shoulders bunching and muscles rippling.

I fly through the trees, hearing him crash through the vegetation. I stop and take a quick right. Hercules slams into the tree beside me. Luckily, this huge animal isn't as limber or agile as a real tiger, or I'd have no chance at getting away. I am only spared because it took him a split second longer to regroup after his massive weight threw him off balance.

I search for a tree with low limbs, and within seconds I'm climbing frantically to the top. I reach a higher branch when Hercules springs off the ground. I jerk my foot out of the way before he can swipe off my leg. His paw nicks the bottom of my shoe. He flashes his giant, vampirish fangs and whisks his tail. The liger springs again, this time almost reaching me barely balancing on the limb. He huffs in frustration.

We both know I'm safe. For now.

Frustrated, he stretches up and expels a deep guttural

growl that is soul shaking. The sound literally makes my bones quiver under my skin. His forearms reach up for one last attempt. His razor-sharp, retractile claws poke out of their furry pouches, hoping to rip me apart. The liger stares with amber eyes that reflect an implacable hatred and hunger.

This animal doesn't play around. He's built to kill.

As the liger paces under me, I sigh a huge breath of temporary relief.

I made it. For now.

I sit up on the limb and wait for the bloodthirsty animal to surrender and go away. He's probably been stalking me for a while, treading silently. I assume no men are with him, or I would have heard them by now. Hopefully Hercules isn't going to tree me until Uncle Bob arrives.

Eventually the adrenaline rush is over, but my body pays the lasting price of its fatigue. Muscles locked. Mouth dry. Brain tired.

As the day winds down, the night noises jump into a whole different symphony. After the last year, the wilderness is no longer a safe refuge for me, a place of beauty and mystique. The way it used to be.

For me, danger lurks everywhere. I never cared what was out in the wilderness with me. But now, as I wait, the thick canopy presses down, suffocating me.

Soon, there's no light left. No matter how much I want to leave, I need to wait it out until morning.

Out here, one wrong move can throw you off.

One wrong move can prove dangerous.

I think about my friends and wonder where they are. *If* Dylan and Sadie are alive, maybe they are perched in a similar tree, thinking about me. I wonder if they feel as alone as I do.

As the night lengthens, shadows and fear consume my

courage, causing pure, unadulterated fear to multiply inside, invading my hope.

I may have gotten this far.

But this is not over yet.

I settle into a crook of the tree and tie myself to a branch with the rope so I don't fall off while I'm asleep.

Tomorrow morning, I need to make a new plan.

SURVIVAL SKILL #13

In a survival situation, open wounds are serious due to tissue damage, blood loss and possible infection. Try to protect them with the proper dressing.

My eyes jerk open.

The woods around me are quiet and the sun hides.

It takes me a second to piece the puzzle together of what's happened over the last twenty-four hours.

I stand in the tree and search the area below me. Hercules is gone and there's no one around. My bionic senses tune into the woods.

It's now or never.

I climb down the tree and hide for a few minutes, waiting. The whole time scanning the trees. Goatees of moss hang from the trees and sway in the hot breeze. The sounds of things skittering catch my attention.

I take out my knife and walk. This time I'm prepared if Hercules—or any animal—attacks. As I travel deeper into the Everglades, the ground grows sloshy. My shoes sink in the sludge but my footprints fill with water, creating little muddy pools. Each step makes a sucking sound. It's like walking on a sponge. Huge buzzing clouds of gnats, mosquitos, and god knows what else think I'm the afternoon buffet.

Another crack of a stick sends me slogging into a deep swamp of water.

The Everglades is a far cry from the Smoky Mountains.

For every tree in the mountains, there is an alligator in the swamps.

As I slog through the hip-deep water, my heartbeat sloshes in my ears. I'm on high alert, sifting through the creepy sounds. The chirp of a tree frog, the hammering of the woodpecker, and the slosh of a turtle sliding into the murky water.

Every splash still sends my heart skittering like a water bug. No matter what the sound is, my mind always thinks one thing...*alligators*.

I take another step and pull my body through the thick but lukewarm water.

If I could find Dylan and Sadie, I'd have a better chance of surviving this mess. But right now, I don't have a fair shot. Being alone out here, the odds are stacked against me.

I bite my bottom lip to keep from crying and slip through the slime and sludge. My knees tremble with every uncertain step I take toward the far embankment. My feet trudge through the heavy silt blanketing the swampy floor. Only a few more yards and I'll finally be back on dry land. I need to get out of this water or I'll surely get a nasty case of trench foot.

A low, growling noise stops me in my tracks. I stop in mid-stride and grip my stick with both hands, knuckles white from squeezing. Alligators make low, growling noises, sounding like a really pissed off lion or tiger. And it's one of the scariest—most horrifying—sounds I've ever heard. Especially when it's nearing dusk and I'm standing in dark water that is now chest deep.

With arms raised in a striking position, I scan the black

water, half-expecting a huge gator to snatch me from underwater and drag me down into the murky abyss.

I hold my breath and wait for another sound to break the silence.

After a few seconds, I wade forward one step at a time. Any step I take could be my last. And I wouldn't see an attack until it was too late. Not knowing what's watching me or where it's hiding gives terror permission to sneak in and choke out each breath, making it shallow and erratic. Even though I want so much to rush, get the hell out of this swamp, I fight against my instinct and work hard to keep my pace slow and even.

Finally, I reach the thin shore but I'm not out of the swamps yet. I jam my stick into the soft, silty mud and grab a low hanging vine. Slowly, I try to pull myself out of the water. My legs grow heavy, weighted down from water-logged pants and soaking wet hiking shoes.

I yank and pull and push until finally I'm free. Once I'm on shore, I scoot away from the water's edge and lean against a dead cypress tree to catch my breath. I scan the still horizon of the water's glassy surface, searching for any sign of a predator. Bubbles. Ripples. Glowing eyes.

I push up to my feet and fight my way up the steep and slippery hill. The whole time I'm periodically scanning the water behind me for any signs of a last minute attack. Out here, you can never let your guard down. Not even for a split second.

Animals wait for it.

Behind me, a few gunshots sound off in the distance.

I dive into the thick underbrush to hide.

This sick game of cat and mouse has gone on long enough.

Something rustles through the bushes across the path from me.

I grab my stick and get ready for anything. Or anyone. If something charges me, I can't hesitate. If I do, it could be the difference between me dying or them.

If given a chance, it's better to kill than be killed. Not a motto I choose to live by but one that has been forced upon me over the last year.

Ahead of me, something slides through the thick vegetation.

I reach into my boot and draw out the large knife Tommy gave me last year for my birthday. Feeling the weight of the steel makes me feel safe. With a weapon in each hand, I back down the path.

When nothing follows, I spin around and stare into the yellow eyes of a huge tan cat. Light-colored slender body, eyes rimmed in thick black lines, and very sharp fangs.

A Florida panther. It's definitely not my Cat, but it means more are out here.

I freeze in my spot and keep my breath shallow. The animal is pretty, sleek, and those eyes could send you into a trance. It makes me happy to know Cat is not alone, though I know there aren't too many left.

The animal growls again.

I keep my head down but I don't dare take my eyes off it. Partly because it's beautiful and partly because it's endangered. But mostly, because it just might pounce.

The panther gives a low warning and flattens its ears against its round shaped head. Eventually it runs off and I exhale.

Something crashes through the woods and I position myself.

In case the panther is coming back.

Suddenly, Sadie's head pops out of the bushes. Dirt on her face, twigs in her hair, and determination on her face.

I cry out, "Sadie!"

She swings around in my direction. When she sees me, she throws her arms in the air. "It's about freakin' time, Grace."

I rush out of the greenery and hug her.

She calls out, "Psst. Dylan, I found her."

A noise thunders through the trees. Dylan's head floats above the bushes until his whole body appears on the path.

"Thank God." He races over and picks me up, swinging me in a circle. "You okay?"

He practically squeezes me to death. "Me? I was worried about you two."

When he places me on the ground, I hug him as Sadie squeezes my hand. "How'd you guys find me?" I try not to sound too disappointed. If they found me, it means I'm being careless.

"We've been trying to track you." Dylan says. "You don't move in a straight line, do you?"

It's official. I've lost my edge.

"You sure the men didn't follow *you*?" I scan the woods, searching for a sign of them.

"Positive." Sadie scoffs. "Though I kinda wish Bob did."

By studying the condition of their lips, I can tell they haven't had much water. I hand her mine. "Here, drink this."

She puts the water to her mouth and takes a sip. Relief passes over her face. She wipes her mouth. "Thanks."

"I thought you guys went in different directions. How did you get to each other?" I ask.

She passes the canteen to Dylan, who takes a quick small sip. "The minute I hit the trees, I beelined in Dylan's direction. Just in time to see him get shot."

My stomach drops at the word. I whip my head around toward him. "Shot? You got shot?"

He points to a piece of cloth tied around his thigh. "It's a flesh wound."

But the amount of blood soaking through the wrap paints a different picture. I throw down my bag and pull out my first aid kit. "Let me see."

Dylan keeps his leg straight as he sits on a fallen dead tree.

I peel off the bandage. It takes everything I have to not to gag. The wound is already infected, with pus and goop oozing out of it. Normally, he'd be fine. But this is the worst environment to get any kind of open injury. The chance for infection is extremely high. If Dylan doesn't get some antibiotics soon, he could be in serious trouble.

Sadie peeks over my shoulder. "Is he okay?"

"Doesn't look too bad." I lie because she doesn't want to hear the real truth. I can tell by her tone, she already knows it's not good. I change the subject to mask my concern as I treat the wound the way Dad taught me. "Where'd the guys go?"

Sadie sits Indian-style on the ground next to me. "Hopefully off to hell."

Dylan winces when I press gauze against his leg. "I saw two go after Sadie. Guess she lost them when she doubled back to find me."

Sadie holds Dylan's hand in comfort. "We lost the one that went after Dylan."

I scan the trees again. "So we could still have some followers."

"Doubt it." Dylan shrugs. "We've been looping around so they couldn't follow."

I pour alcohol on clean gauze and gently touch it to his leg. Dylan grunts and stiffens. "Oh, stop being a baby. Sadie, hold this for a second." I tape the cloth to his leg and grab her hand to hold it in place.

I take out a black garbage bag and tear off a piece, wrapping it over the bandage and around his thigh. Hopefully the plastic will protect the wound. Keep the water and other nasty stuff out. Hopefully, we won't be stuck out here too long.

When I'm done, I bury the bloody cloth. Don't want to attract animals or leave a trace.

Dylan inspects his injury. "Thanks. Hey, what about you? How'd you get away?"

I plop down on my butt and sigh, thinking of Annie. "I snuck by the liger. He was eating..."

Sadie shakes her head as if what I am saying is not true. "Annie? Oh God, that's horrible! Poor thing. Her parents have been searching everywhere for her. They're going to be devastated. Wonder if the other kid is out here somewhere." She glances around.

"I haven't seen him." I say. Or his body for that matter. It's been a long time since the boy disappeared so that's what I would expect to find out here. A body. And in this place, he'll probably never show up. Lost forever. Leaving a family always wondering why he left. At least I can give Annie's parents closure. It's the only thing that got me past finding Dad and then losing him. Knowing is better than not knowing. No matter how painful.

I imagine Annie lying there and hold back tears. I spare Dylan and Sadie the gory details and fill in blanks. "The liger followed me. Tried to eat me. I had to sleep in a tree. That's why I was hiding when you guys showed up."

"Because ligers don't search in hiding places?" Dylan smirks when he says it.

I'm frustrated, tired, and scared, so his remarks make me mad. "I'm sorry...when did this all become funny, Dylan? A girl died. In front of us. And we have very little time to get the hell out of here or these crazy guys are going to hunt us down and kill us. Not to mention you're wounded, alerting every hungry animal to our presence."

Dylan holds up his hands. "Okay sorry."

Sadie punches him in the arm and scowls. "She's right. This is serious. We need to blow this popsicle stand so I can hang this guy for life. I'll be dang if I'm letting him take me out or get away with what he did to Annie...and God knows who else."

"We need to keep heading east as long as there's light. We camp at night." Out here, it's too dangerous in the dark. You never know when animals or swamps will pop up.

Dylan pushes up to his feet and wobbles. I find him a walking stick, which at first he refuses. Like he's too tough for nature's cane.

"Hold it for me then." I lead the group forward. Me in the front with Sadie and Dylan behind me. Every few feet, I glance back at them. She has her arm wrapped around his waist as he limps along the path. Every now and then he shoos her away. Because he can do it himself. But like a loyal dog, she always ventures back to his side.

We walk along the path, parallel to the swamp.

I keep my eye on the water. We definitely don't want to travel close to that any longer than we have too.

Dylan stops and stands at the swamp's edge, looking at the murky water. "Man, I'm so hungry, I'd probably eat an alligator right now."

"That's awful." Sadie slaps his back. "You wouldn't."

I pull my last granola bar out of my bag and hand it to Dylan. When he protests, I insist. "You need your strength."

A few alligators surface in the water as if they heard his threat.

She points at the small army. "I think they feel the same about you."

"Guys!" I spin around and face them, fists balled. "This is not Survivor. This is serious."

Dylan waves me off. "Come on, Grace. Those men are jokes so I'm not afraid."

Sadie's eyes are wide but she doesn't take either side.

"Maybe you should be," I snap back, my face heating up either from my below-the-surface-anger or high humidity. "They killed Annie. Without blinking. And they plan on doing the same to us. They won't—no can't—let us get out of here alive or they know we'll talk. We have to stay ahead of them. As much as you know the swamps, they know just as much. This is their turf."

Sadie nods. "Dylan, she's right. No doubt you're tough, but they have numbers going for them. Let's get out of here in one piece. Then we can get our revenge."

A boat motor sputters from the swampy water. Voices come from behind us in the woods. First a murmur then louder and louder.

My heart doesn't know whether to jump or stop.

We have no place to go. They're searching by land and water.

Dylan points at the swamp, motioning for us to follow. The three of us wade into the murky water and sink up to our chests. I try to drown my fear. The men aren't the only threat. We hide behind a clump of mangroves and cattails.

"Over here. I got me a track!"

Dylan whispers as low as he can. "You two need to go. I'll distract these guys."

"That's stupid." Sadie hisses on the s. "We stay together."

He frowns and a serious look crosses his face. I can't tell if it's fear or anger. "I'm in charge. Not you."

"Since when?"

"Since right now." He kisses her forehead. "Now go. Wade that way down the swamp. I'll catch up to you."

I can't help but think about his wound. He shouldn't be in this water at all. "Dylan, let's find another way."

Sadie doesn't say anything but her bottom lip quivers. Sometimes she puts on a tough act because she wants big, bad Dylan to think she's strong.

"Trust me." He hands me his walking stick and sloshes off through the water. Once he's a few yards away, he makes enough splashing noises to catch the hunter's attention. And every alligator within a mile's range.

Eventually, he sinks underneath the reptile and bacteria-ridden water and swims away.

"Hey! Over there. In the water."

Sadie and I remain where we are, holding each other. She's muttering please God over and over until Dylan's head disappears behind a cypress tree.

Uncle Bob's deep voice bellows from the bank. "I want that boy alive. You two keep hiking. The girls are probably close by."

I grab Sadie's hand and tug her behind me. We move through the water. I stare into the darkness, waiting for something to pull me under and drown me. Neither of us speaks for at least a mile.

Finally, she whispers. "You think he's okay?" Her voice trembles on each word. It's the first time she sounds a little broken.

"I hope so." I say, keeping my voice strong and solid. For her.

But inside, I'm asking myself the same question.

And I'm not feeling good about my answer.

SURVIVAL SKILL #14

If you are bitten by a venomous snake, stay calm. If not, your heart will beat faster, which increases the flow of blood to the bite and the amount of toxin into the tissues.

Sadie and I leave Dylan behind.

Something we both already regret.

Even though we don't say it, deep down we are both worried Dylan may not make it.

That he sacrificed himself for us.

We push through the mud and plants. My legs cramp from the resistance and feel heavy from my pants being weighed down. I keep Dylan's stick out in front of me, waiting to defend us if an alligator should pop up, wanting a mid-day meal.

As we glide through the water, it becomes shallower, though it's still too risky to creep up on the path. Every now and then, we hear an occasional gun shot or yell in the distance.

She whimpers behind me but I don't dare look back. "You okay?" I ask over my shoulder.

"No." Sadie sniffs. "We never should have let him go alone."

I agree but don't say that. "He'll be fine. If he can beat out all those alligators, these men won't pose a problem."

"I hope you're right, Grace. Because I'm starting to wonder if we're ever going to get out of here. Alive"

I stop and turn around. Sadie's eyes are swollen and red. I touch her shoulder. "Sadie, you have to stay positive. If we let this get our spirits down, the chances of us not making it get bigger. We need to keep moving."

She nods and wipes her face with her shoulder. "Okay."

Sadie and I slide across the swamp, wading through clumps of floating lily pads and vegetation. Even though the water is only up to our knees now, gators and snakes are still a huge threat. They can hide in only a foot of water. And a small gator can do more damage than anyone ever expects. Even though I'm terrorized by not knowing what is beneath me, I push on.

Today, the sun blazes overhead so the water is a bit welcoming. If it wasn't for what lurked beneath.

Sadie and I go back to being silent. It's safer that way.

Which leaves me at the mercy of my racing mind.

All I can think about is how worried Birdee must be. Plus I'm sure she's called my mom by now. Can't imagine what Mom's going through. Again. Wonder if Mo knows we're missing. And if he does, will he come down to help find us? If not, I hope someone's out searching.

I hear a motor.

I glance back and spot a boat moving slowly in our direction.

"Move!" I hiss back at Sadie. She sloshes through the water behind me until I spot a bank to climb. "There!"

When I reach the edge, I grab the mangrove roots and pull my waterlogged body out of the stinky water. I turn and help Sadie out.

A man shouts, "There they are!"

The boat motor speeds up and groans louder as it glides closer.

A shot rings out. Sadie and I duck into the cover of the mangroves. The roots create cages around us. Bullets rip through leaves behind us as we push and squeeze through the vegetation like Br'er Rabbit in the briar patch. Thick roots grab at our hair and wrap around our legs, trying to hold us back. The Everglades shows no mercy to visitors.

When the shots stop, Sadie calls out to me, grunting. "You think they'll follow us?"

"I don't see how," I say, jerking a vine off my leg. "We can barely get through, and they're twice our size. But keep an eye out. This may dump us back at the water and they'll be waiting somewhere."

She yelps in pain, which sends my heart reeling.

I spin around. "What happened?"

Her face is pale and she's staring down into the water. "I...I think something bit me."

I spot a ripple. A three-foot snake skims across the top of the water, racing toward me. I grab the roots and pull myself out of the water just as it passes under me. I poke it with a stick and it opens its white mouth.

A cottonmouth.

My heart tanks. Birdee has warned me many times about these snakes.

Sadie panics. "Grace? What is it? Is it bad?"

After it passes, I drop into the water and slog back to her. I work to keep her calm even though the pit of my stomach aches. "It's okay Sadie. Let's get out and take a look." But deep down, my inner voice yells: *this is not good. This is not good.*

I clutch her arm and lift her leg out of the water. "Keep it high until we reach land." I pull her to a break in the roots and drag her up on the silky mud.

She throws her arm over my shoulder and I lead her up onto the moist path. I sit her down against a tree and drop to my knees. My waterproof bag drips on the outside, but inside everything is still dry.

I pull out my kit and cut back her pant leg. Blood trickles from two small teeth marks. The area around the bite is already red and swollen. This tells me a lot. The snake is venomous and the venom is acting fast.

Sadie whimpers when she sees the wound. "This is bad isn't it?"

I touch the side of her calf, where blood spurts out of two tiny holes. "Don't panic, Sadie. That's the worst thing you can do. It forces the venom into your bloodstream faster. Stay calm okay? You're going to be fine."

I try to remember what Dad taught visitors about snakebites. Ideally, medical attention and anti-venom are the best way to offset the venom. But out here, what other choice do I have?

I can't sit here and do nothing.

Sadie starts to shiver. Snakebites resemble septic shock and this is the first sign that the venom is attacking the tissue. I have no choice but to attempt to suck out the venom, then tourniquet her leg. It the only option I have. And it's not a good one.

I sit back on my heels. "Okay. Listen, here's the deal. Because of the color and swelling, it was probably a cottonmouth."

"That's not good, right?"

I try to smile. "It's not great. But think how much you will impress Dylan.

"Okay."

"Sadie, you're going to be fine, I promise. I'm going to try and suck out some venom but we may have to wait this out. Together."

Tears stream down her cheeks and she nods. "I trust you."

"Good, because I'm all you got right now." I grab my first

aid kit and clean the outside with an alcohol wipe. I try to mentally prepare for the gross deed. The deed that has little chance of saving her life. The deed I have to do.

"Now. This is going to hurt a little."

I press on her leg and use Tommy's knife to slice a small incision across the wound.

She yelps and bites on her shirt. "Thought you said a little."

"I lied." I give her a pouty lip. "Sorry. You ready?"

She shakes her head no as sweat beads trickle down her face.

"Too bad. Here goes." I pinch the wound and put my lips on her leg. I suck out a small bit of blood and liquid then spit it off to the side. My stomach flips a few times, getting queasy, but I push on. I'd rather throw up than let my friend die. I repeat the sucking and spitting a few times and then wash my mouth out with water. Even though venom is only activated through blood, extra caution can't hurt.

By now, Sadie is in full-blown shock and pain. I lay her back on my plastic poncho and prop her leg up on a small log. I take off her shoes and mine. If I don't dry them all out, we will get a bad case of trench foot from the water soaking through our socks. To minimize the smoke, I dig a hole in the ground and start a fire. I check to make we're not sending out a signal to the men. I place our shoes and socks next to the hole. Then I stretch out my white, wrinkly feet, letting the warmth dry them out.

I sit quietly next to Sadie and check her wound periodically. Her leg is still swelling. Most likely what I did won't have any effect, but I don't know what else to do.

She cries out in pain a couple of times. I hold her hand and let her squeeze. To keep her from yelling and attracting Uncle Bob's men, I give her stick to bite down on. If they find us, we're both dead.

The whole night, Sadie shows symptoms of a bad bite. Pain, swelling, shivering. Large dark blisters show up around the bite mark. At one point, her breathing grows labored. Doesn't surprise me. The cottonmouth's venom can cause serious tissue damage and force a body to shut down.

Now there's nothing to do but wait.

And hope.

And pray.

I rest my head against the tree and focus on the best outcome possible. Sadie will come out of this - probably deeply scarred - but alive. She has to.

Yet, a small piece of my brain can't help but slide to a popular outcome in my life.

Death.

It's natural. But, for some reason, it loves hanging around me. First Dad then Seth. Hopefully, Sadie breaks my running streak.

Sadie cries throughout the night.

I comfort her by whispering in her ear, "You're going to be okay, Sadie. I promise."

A promise I can't keep. One I have no control over.

I don't even know if she hears me anymore.

By midnight, her eyes roll back into her head, and even though her spasms have waned some, her leg continues to swell. And her pain appears to get worse.

As the sky darkens, my eyes struggle to stay open. I'm afraid to go to sleep but the adrenaline of the day has worn down my body.

My eyes close, and I pray Sadie's still alive when I open them in the morning.

SURVIVAL SKILL #15

Saw grass has sharp, saw-teeth along the blades that cut like razors. You have to protect your arms, face and legs or you will get cut.

The next morning when I open my eyes, Sadie's back is toward me. I can't see her face.

My heart pounds in my chest. I'm afraid to move. Afraid to look.

I sit still for several seconds, hoping to hear her breathe.

I remember the day I found Seth in the woods. He froze to death after being outside in the worst snowstorm in North Carolina history. Even though we eventually discovered he was murdered. I'll never forget the exact second I realized he was dead. Feeling helpless and guilty all at the same time. Whether it was my fault or not.

I suck in a deep breath and lightly shake her shoulder. My voice tries to hide in my throat so I whisper, "Sadie?"

She rolls over to face me. Her voice comes out weak and scratchy. "Hey."

"Hey yourself." I smile and bend over to hug her. Tears shed from my eyes as relief pours over me. Sadie's alive, and I'm thankful. She's still in danger, but at least she survived the worst part—the first night. Even though she's talking and coherent, it's still critical that I get her to a hospital. Only now, the dangers are not as life threatening. She may have permanent tissue damage on her leg, but if I can get her medical attention, it might save her leg.

At least she is alive.

I take out my water and hold it to her pale lips.

She takes a few sips.

"How do you feel?"

"Like shit. How do you think I feel?"

I can't help but smile. Sadie is feistier than any nasty snake I've ever encountered.

I remove the dressing on her leg and inspect the bite. Gross, it still looks nasty. Dark purple and swollen with goo.

"Gross." Sadie winces when I touch the wound. "Shitake, it hurts like nobody's business."

"You're lucky that sucker didn't release more." I rewrap her leg with a strip of gauze. "By the size of the snake, you could have died."

She sits up and watches me pack up our stuff, getting rid of any trace we were here. "Leaving so soon?"

"We need to go. Now. You need anti-venom."

"Not sure I'm ready to leave." She winks. "It's so fun here."

I stare at her with no expression. "I'm serious."

"So am I?" She grits her teeth in pain. "I don't know about you but I'm going to complain to the travel agent. This place sucks."

I can't help but smile. "Great. At least you kept your sense of humor. But if we don't leave, you could lose some of your leg. Just sayin'."

"You don't hold back do you?" She narrows her eyes and wears a smirk. "I like that."

"Nope." I rip open a tiny emergency pack of Ibuprofen with my teeth. "Take this."

She sits up and swallows the two pills dry. "Pretty sure I need something a little stronger."

"Sorry, pharmacy is closed." I fish through my bag and pull out the leftover garbage bag I used on Dylan and some fishing wire. "Hold still. I need to protect this wound or you could die of a nasty infection."

Sadie cracks up at this. "Jesus. That would totally suck. Get bit by a three-foot cottonmouth, go through a crap-load of pain, only to make it and then die of a dumb infection."

After I wrap her whole calf, I clutch her hand and pull her to her feet. As soon as she puts pressure on her leg, she yelps in pain.

I hand her my walking stick. "This won't be easy."

"I like hard," Sadie says.

"Come on. We don't have much time." I grab my backpack and throw it over my shoulder. I study my compass. "If we go north, we should get out of the swamps and back on dry land. I hope."

As I turn to walk off, Sadie grabs my arm.

When I turn to face her, she presses her lips together, as if she's trying not to cry. "Thank you."

I grin. "You're welcome. But don't get too excited until you see my bill."

Sadie jumps on me and squeezes me tight. "I mean it. You're a good friend, Grace. I owe you."

It takes me a few seconds to accept the hug. I've never had huggy friends before. I've seen them at school. The pack of girls who hug every time they see each other. Between classes, after classes, after school, before lunch. I've just never been included. Wyn's the only solid friend I've had back home and his hugs have been filled with tension since we broke up. Now, there is always a strange barrier between us.

I hug Sadie back. "You're welcome. Now let's get out of here."

"I second that."

Sadie leans on me as we move through the mangroves

and into a prairie field filled with communities of saw grass fighting off herds of cattails. In some places, the ground is covered with an inch of slushy algae. In others, the water is much deeper, leading into huge ponds. In the distance, I spot more pine trees flanked by more swamps.

The urge to run grows. I hate being out in the open. Even though the saw grass reaches the top of my head, the idea that I can't hide or climb anywhere makes me anxious. I'm also aware those men could be hiding and we wouldn't see them until it was too late.

"Let's hurry." I can hear the urgency cutting through my voice.

Sadie hobbles behind me, mumbling. "Easy for you to say."

We walk and walk through the thick saw grass. I hold a walking stick out in front of me, pressing down on the bladed grass, but it still slices through my skin like a thousand paper cuts. A few times, one catches me in the cheek.

Sadie follows close behind and grunts every time one cuts her arm.

A thumping noise off to my right. I stop and listen as it grows louder and louder.

I stiffen to brace myself, knowing something's going to happen.

Out of nowhere, something jumps out of the grass and slams into me. Sadie screams when I drop to the ground. It only takes me seconds to pop up to my feet with my knife already drawn.

A young boy is in the same stance as me. I recognize him immediately. Junior is what Bob called him. This kid's the one that chickened out of shooting game. The kid that refused to shoot Annie.

I drop my guard a little, hoping I can reason with him. "What are you doing here?"

Before I can say anything to persuade him from hurting us, he lunges at me and grabs both my arms. "Pa, I got them!"

So much for negotiation.

I stomp down hard on his foot. He grunts and lets go. His mistake gives me enough time to spin around and jab him in the throat. He makes a gurgling sound and stumbles backward, clawing at his throat to catch a breath.

Sadie approaches the kid who's flailing on the ground.

I yell at her. "Get out of here!"

She ignores me and stands over the boy, whose menacing look has morphed into pure fear. This kid is harmless. She points at a necklace around his neck. "Where the F did you get that?"

The boy doesn't answer; he's still trying to catch his breath.

When I focus in, I now notice the necklace is Dylan's. Sadie is about to flip out; it's all over her face. "Sadie? I got this."

She screams. "Where did you get that?"

I touch her arm and she flinches. "Sadie, go. I'll get it back. I promise."

I can tell she's confused, like it's all processing in her head. But she surrenders and her body goes limp. "You better, Grace."

"Hurry, you need the head start."

Even though Sadie's in major pain, she picks up her stick and goes half running, half hopping across the field, disappearing into the tall grass.

Then man calls out again, this time he sounds closer. "Junior! Answer me!"

The boy pushes to his feet and lunges at me, catching me off totally by surprise. I jump out of the way at the last minute.

He tries to pull a gun out of his belt but I see it coming and kick it from his hands. The weapon flies into the weeds.

I regain my fighting stance, holding out my knife, and eye the dangling alligator claw. "Where'd you get that?"

The boy sneers. "From your friend. Trust me, he wasn't as strong as he looked." Then the dumb kid attacks me again, refusing to give up.

Anger heats my adrenaline and it boils over. I lash out, landing a direct punch to his mouth. He doesn't even stagger. Instead, he hits me back right in the jaw. I stumble back a few steps, stunned. Spots wiggle in my vision and I drop to my knees. Tommy's knife shoots out of my hand. Vision foggy, I scramble across the ground before he sees it and grab it. Then I roll over on my back as the boy jumps.

He falls on top of me and his eyes go wide. His body stiffens.

Then he goes limp.

I roll out from under him and stand to face him. But he doesn't get up as fast as I expect.

That's when I notice the blood on my knife and hands. When I focus, the boy lies in the grass. A pool of blood circles him. Both his hands cover the stomach wound as he tries to stop the bleeding.

It takes a second for it all to hit me. Then panic settles in. I drop next to him and I fumble with my pack. I pull out an old shirt and press the cloth to his stomach. "Oh my God."

The boy's eyes are wide and fearful.

I start to cry. Tears fall on his face. "I'm so sorry. I didn't mean to..."

Someone yells again. "Junior!"

"It's okay. My fault." The boy looks at me. Blood trickles from the side of his mouth. His voice gurgles with liquid. "I'm dying."

I lean down and whisper. "No. You're going to be okay...I promise." The same promise I can't keep.

The boy shakes his head and tries to talk but nothing comes out. I recognize the look in his eyes. The same look Dad had before he died. And just like Dad, this boy knows he's dying too.

I lean over him and press harder but the blood won't stop. It's too much. Tears blur my vision. I've killed some poor kid and I never wanted to hurt anyone.

The boy opens his mouth again.

I lean down to try and make out his words.

He chokes out one raspy, gurgled word, "Run."

Something crashes through the weeds, moving closer.

When I look back down, the boy is dead. His eyes wide as they stare at the sky.

I kiss his forehead and close his eyes. Then I take Dylan's necklace and stuff it in my pocket. I jump up and bolt the clearing. I sob as I race for the trees, running faster than ever.

Away from something I will always regret.

Away from the biggest mistake of my whole life.

Away from a vengeful father who is about to find his dead son.

The son I killed.

SURVIVAL SKILL #16

If you are with another person or a group, you should always stay together. Do not separate, do not split up, and never move out too far away from each other.

The breath in my ears doesn't drown out the words I'm screaming in my head.

I killed that boy. I killed that boy.

I hear the man yell when he finds his son. His screams are followed by gunshots. Bullets spray around me, exploding dirt and clumps of grass.

I zigzag and spot Sadie way ahead, waving me on. She holds out her hand, waiting for me to catch up.

I reach out and grab it. The two of us race through the field, hand in hand. No girl left behind.

A few stray pine trees offer little shelter from any animal or madman. We scramble into a clump of palms and stop.

I lean over and press my hands against my knees to catch my breath.

Sadie gasps, "Oh my god. You're hurt."

That's when I notice I'm covered in blood. My hands. My shirt. My pants. I frantically wipe my hands on my pants as Sadie fusses over me.

"Are you okay? What happened? Where is it coming from?"

I push her away from me. "Stop! It's not mine!" My voice comes out louder than I intend.

Sadie freezes. She appears horrified and retreats a few paces. "Grace? Whose blood is it?"

Jerking a bandana out of my bag, I bend over a puddle and frantically wash my hands. The water turns from a muddy brown to a bright red.

"Grace?" Sadie says. Her voice is slow and deliberate as if she's choosing her words carefully. "What happened back there?"

I freeze, hunched over, and hang my head. My reflection stares back. A stranger. The horrific scene replays in my mind. The boy attacking me. Me grabbing the knife. The boy jumping on me. And then, all the blood. His words haunt me. *Run!* Even after I hurt him, even knowing he was about to die, he tried to warn me. Protect me from getting hurt.

I can hear his voice as if he's next to me. *Run!*

When the movie ends, it replays all over again. Though the edges and details are foggy. None of this makes sense. Like it didn't really happen.

"Grace?" This time Sadie's voice is calm. Her hand touches my shoulder.

"I killed him." I shake my head as tears stream down my face. "I didn't mean to." I can't stop wiping my hands. Over and over. But they won't get clean. "He just kept coming."

She squats next to me and grabs both of my hands to stop me from scraping on my own skin. "It's okay."

I glance at her through blurry eyes. "Is it? Because I don't think it is." I dry my hands on my pants but they're still tinged pink, reminding me of what I've done. Not that I will ever forget.

"He jumped you. I saw him. He would have killed you."

My lips don't seem to form any words, but I hear them

pour out. "I fell. The knife popped out of my hands. I grabbed it but..." My voice fades.

Sadie doesn't say a word. Her expression doesn't even change. She has no judgment. No questions. She just listens.

I muster up the energy to finish. "He jumped on me, and I...I didn't mean to, but he landed on top of me. The knife was in my hand. I think I held it out in instinct but I'm not really sure what happened..."

"It's not your fault." Sadie lifts my face to her level. "What else were you supposed to do Grace? It was him or you."

I sit back on my butt and bury my face in my hands. "I killed him and then he said he was sorry. To me. I killed him and he apologizes. How did this happen? I can't even kill a cockroach."

Sadie frowns. "Look, it sucks that kid is dead. But these guys started all this. A bunch of backwoods freaks kidnap us and drag us out in the boonies. Then they let us go, hunt us down. They sic some mutant tiger on some poor girl and probably killed the boy that's still missing. And that's who we know of. As far as I'm concerned, you did what you had to do...to survive."

"Maybe." I wipe my eyes with the back of my hand. The only part that isn't stained pink with blood. "But that means I'm no better than any of them."

She shrugs. "You didn't kill that kid in cold blood. Even after he attacked you, you tried to warn him. Asked him to stay away. I heard you. But he just kept coming."

A deep yell breaks my trance. "If you find her, I want that girl myself."

Sadie and I peer over the tall grass. She teeters on her feet and falls backward like she's going to pass out. I catch her and help her sit down on the ground.

"Hey? You okay?"

She holds her head between her knees. "I'm fine. Just a little dizzy."

"That's normal. Let me see." I make her turn away and check her leg. If she sees how bad it looks, she's going to freak out. The bite is black and purple and very swollen with large nasty white blisters. She'll probably lose a good chunk of her leg. I quickly rewrap it and secure the plastic bag. "We have to get you out of here."

"But they're still coming."

I watch the grass, listening for any movement the men are moving in our direction. The boy's face fills my mind—eyes open, gawking at the sky, as if he was hoping that's where he would go. I'll never forgive myself. Justified or not, I took someone's life. A kid. Someone's son. Probably someone's brother.

A lump forms in my throat. "I didn't even know his name."

Sadie rubs my back. "Would that have made a difference?"

"I guess not, but it feels so personal. I should have asked." A gunshot cracks in the distance. "And that poor boy's dad is mad as hell. I killed his kid. He'll never let up on me now."

"Grace?" Sadie whispers. "For all you know, they killed Dylan.

I snap my head in her direction.

She stares at the ground and picks a weed.

"Why do you say that?"

She rolls her eyes. "Please. I saw Dylan's necklace around that boy's neck. I gave it to him. I'd know it anywhere."

I pat my pocket and pull out the alligator claw. I'd almost forgotten it. "I got it back for you."

"Thank you." She holds out her hand and I drop it in her palm. She stares at it and tears fill her eyes, but they never fall.

"I'm sure he's fine." I say. "He's strong. You know that."

She wipes her eyes and shakes her head. "I don't know. He'd never let anyone take this necklace."

"Maybe it fell off."

She glances at me with narrow eyes. "We both know that didn't happen."

The next gunshot is louder. Closer. They're gaining on us.

"We have to go."

Sadie shakes her head no.

"Sadie, we have to go."

"I can't." She ties the black cord around her neck and strokes the alligator claw with her fingers. "I need to go find Dylan."

I shake my head hard and tug on her arm to get her to stand. "No. That's impossible."

"It wasn't a question." Sadie pulls my hand off her bicep. "Grace, I have to do this. I can't leave this hellhole without knowing what happened to him. I have to try."

I shake my head. "You can't. You need to get to a hospital. You could lose part of your leg if you don't get that anti-venom. Cottonmouth bites..."

She holds up one hand to stop my Public Service Announcement against snakes. "I don't care. I love Dylan. He's more important than my stupid leg."

"Fine. Then I'll go with you." I say it, but it's not what I want to do. At. All. "I'm not letting you go on your own."

"No!" She stands and winces. "You need to get back. Nail these bozos. Tell everyone what's going on before some other poor teen who's left home on a whim gets killed."

"Can't leave you out here."

"You're not." Sadie straightens up, trying to act real tough. Though I can see she's hurting. "I'm leaving you."

"Sadie, please. You can't do this. You're hurt."

"Let me ask you something." She presses her lips tight,

telling me she's not going to budge on this decision. "What would you do if it was Mo?"

"What?" The name pricks a hole in my heart. I try not to think about Mo a lot. I miss him so much. More than ever. Especially out here, when he's all I think about. But Sadie and I have never talked about Mo so I wasn't expecting her to bring him up now.

"Dylan's told me how much you love Mo. He said you talk about him all the time. I guess Mo asked Dylan to watch out for you so I know Mo feels the same way about you. What would you do if Mo were out here? Alone. And you thought he might be hurt?"

My body sags. I remember that time it happened. Mo was on the hill and took a bullet for my dad and I didn't want to leave Mo behind. The only reason I did is because my dad was in bad shape and Al was hunting us down. But if Dad wasn't there with me, I never would have left Mo on that hill to die. Not in a million years.

"Well?"

I sigh. "I would have gone looking for him."

"Exactly." The way she says it confirms one thing. Nothing I do or say will change her mind. She's going after Dylan whether she should or not.

"Fine. I'll only let you go on one condition." I pull off my backpack. I take a small string bag and throw in the first aid kit, a protein bar, the canteen, a Swiss Army knife, and a few other useful things she might need. I keep my bag with a bar, water filter kit, and my knife, and hand her the makeshift survival kit. "Take this."

"What if you need it?"

"I won't. I have what I need and if not, I know what to do. My dad taught me a lot. You need this stuff way more than me. Don't forget I'm heading home. You're heading..."

"...Back into hell." She tries to laugh it off but I can see she's scared. "Are you saying your dad can kick my dad's ass?"

I smile. "Definitely."

"You're probably right. But I have Dylan and he's taught me a lot more than you think."

I hold out the pack for her to take. "Stay hydrated and don't forget to keep changing your bandage. There's enough gauze in there to last you. Keep it dry, and if you get an infection...."

"I know. I know." She grabs the string of the pack. "Infection equals bad."

I hug her tight for a few seconds longer than I should and pull back. "Sadie, be careful. Lay low. These guys aren't as dumb as you and Dylan think. I'll send someone after you as soon as I get back." I hand her my compass last. "If you get lost, remember to head due west. You're bound to hit the Gulf at some point."

"What about you?"

"I have my GPS watch." I hold up my wrist to show her. "And my wits."

Sadie smiles, "Oh, well then you are better off than me. I lost mine a long time ago." She turns to walk off. "See you on the other side."

I hold up my hand as she waves. "You better."

Inside, I'm torn. Part of me wants to go with her. Yet, the other part knows I need to get home. This thing isn't over yet. And these men are still hurting people.

I shove my knife into the back of my belt and watch Sadie walk off into the bright sun.

I pray she's right.

I hope I'll see her again.

—————

SURVIVAL SKILL #17

—————

Animal bites are dangerous in two ways. The actual bite causes damage plus it can result in a severe infection.

After Sadie is gone, it takes all my strength to turn around and leave.

I jog into the thicker part of the pinelands, hiding behind trees as I go. A few men are still yelling in the distance. They've obviously joined forces and don't seem to care if they're quiet or not. If I can stay hidden, maybe they'll get bored and go away. Maybe they'll think I'm long gone.

Until the sun sets, I'm a walking beacon. When my foot sinks into another mud puddle, I scoop some into my hands and rub it on my face. Even though it cools down my scorched face, I can't help but cringe at the slimy mud. It will protect my skin and help me blend in more.

My feet squish in the silty ground with an identity crisis between being full-on mud or solid dirt. I check behind me and notice I'm leaving tracks. Luckily, with each step, the footprints flood with mud and water. As if I was never there.

For a while, nothing happens. Just one wet foot in front of another.

Snap.

The sound happens behind me. Too close.

147

I don't even turn around to see who or what it is.

I just run.

It might have been a rabbit or a raccoon. But it doesn't matter. My nerves are so on edge they kick in and send me careening through the thick grass, sharp sticks, and over holes.

A pounding noise holds my attention. It feels like it's on my heels. If I look back, that extra second might cost me. Then barking. Over and over. The sounds grow closer and closer. I can outrun an old man with a gun but not a mean dog on a hunt of a lifetime.

My breath quickens—in and out—I speed up. As fast as my legs can roll under me. I keep all my focus on the woods. Now inching closer and closer. My lungs sear in pain and I think I pulled a hamstring but I keep on. Only a few yards now.

I dart left and right, leaping over palmettos and punches of grass like I'm doing hurdles. Even when my foot slides on a slippery patch, I regain control and keep the pace.

Something hard bites onto the back of my boot. I'm running so fast, I lose control and trip. When I roll over on my back, I'm face to face with some kind of wolf dog. A mix between the beloved gray wolf and a Siberian husky. The dog grabs hold of my shoe and shakes it back and forth, like it's a freakin' squirrel.

Luckily, the leather holds against the strong grip of his teeth.

A man's head appears over the tall grass. He grabs me by the hair and drags me to one side, throwing me up against a tree. My head slams against a root.

The man stands over me. "Gotcha! See if you get away again." His voice is sharp, loud. He's not here to play. He's crazed, his eyes wide with anger.

Suddenly, the wolf dog is in my face, showing his bared

teeth. Breath smells of meat. Little droplets of foam hang from his black lips. The thing is either hot or plain rabid.

"Easy, Spike. Leave some for me." The man's gruff tone makes me think he smokes or strains his voice enough to damage his vocal chords.

The man turns his baseball cap backward and spits a chunk of tobacco. "You hurt my boy."

"I didn't mean to." My hands shake as the image of that poor kid pops in my head. I stare down at my hands and flip them over. They are still stained. "I swear."

"Doesn't do him no good, does it?" The man shrugs. The guy pulls his dog off me. "Get up."

I slowly stand. "Listen, if you let me go, I swear I won't tell a soul about anything that's happened here." I make it to my feet and keep my hands to my side.

The guy eyes me. "Shut up and don't move."

The radio on his hip blurts out static followed by Uncle Bob's voice, "You got her?"

The man grins and holds down the button. "Nope. She got away."

"I want her alive. Got good use for her." Uncle Bob's clicks off and then returns. "Let me know when you find her."

"Will do, boss." The man tucks his radio in his pant pocket and ties his dog to a tree.

"You didn't tell him." I'm confused and not sure what's going on. "You don't want him to kill me?"

He shrugs. "Nope."

I tilt my head. Is it possible this guy might actually let me go? Maybe he's going to take my bogus deal. For a second, I allow hope to return. That is, until he begins loading his gun.

One bullet at a time.

I remain calm with a shred of hope. "So, what are you going to do?"

He laughs as he loads in the last bullet and pops the gun cartridge shut. "Gonna kill you myself. For what you did to my boy."

He raises the gun and points it at my forehead. "Eye for an eye."

Before he can squeeze the trigger, I pull the knife out of my belt and throw it.

The sharp blade tucks into his upper thigh, causing him to drop to the ground. He drops the gun and writhes in the grass.

I stand still as the dog pulls at the leash. Barking. Growling. He kinda reminds me of Bear, Dad's dog that stayed at the ranger station with him and Les. The same dog that took a bullet and died. I haven't forgotten him and I miss him every day.

I remain crouched over as the man grabs his radio.

"I found her! But the little wench knifed me. I'm over at the Bear's Den." He sneers. "She ain't going nowhere. Spike will see to that." The guy sits up, holding his leg. The dog yanks and thrashes at the leash, waiting for the release. He reaches over and works to untie Spike's rope. "I dare you to run."

I take a step back, wondering if he's right, and kick something. When I glance over, the gun sits in a clump of weeds. I slowly bend down and brush the gun with my fingers.

"Get her, Spike." He frees the dog and it comes bounding toward me.

I pick up the gun and point the weapon at the dog. I don't know if I can kill something else. Mean dog or not. The weapon quivers as my hand shakes.

The man struggles to stand, now afraid for his dog's life. "Attack! Spike. Attack!"

Spike races toward me and launches himself in the air.

I have the perfect shot, but I can't muster up enough will to fire.

The large dog's front paws hit my chest, pushing me to the ground. His heavy body lands on top of mine, knocking the wind from me. I can barely catch a breath before his jaws snap in my face. I grab the dog's neck with both hands and hold his mouth away. His weight presses down on my arms that threaten to crumple.

I can smell his breath. Rancid. Hot. Smells of beef jerky.

We roll around on the ground and he catches my forearm in his jaws.

I yelp out in pain as the man laughs in the background. "Nobody messes with Spike."

I pull my fist back and punch the dog square in the nose.

It yelps once but attacks again. Pain is not a problem.

A rustling noise breaks out behind me and I hear the man yell at someone, "Hey!"

Then a gun shot.

The dog goes limp and collapses on my chest.

I sit up and push the carcass off me. My chest heaves with adrenaline mixed with hysteria. My arm throbs from the bite. I push through the pain and stand as a figure steps out of the shadows.

I squint. The bright sun hangs directly above me, distorting my vision.

The shadow walks toward me.

My heart skips.

I would recognize that walk anywhere.

"Mo?"

I run toward Mo.

But when I pass the man, he grabs my foot from the ground and trips me.

I fall forward and catch myself with both hands.

Mo leaps over me like I'm a log and decks the guy in the face while he's still in mid-air. "Don't touch her!"

The guy doesn't even get a chance to fight back. He goes limp and falls back in the weeds.

Mo rushes to my side and checks me out. "You okay, Blossom?"

"I am now." I wrap my arms around his neck and squeeze him tight. It feels like forever since I held him. His familiar scent returns and the last month of tension left from being apart shrinks. "What are you doing here?"

"Looking for you." He pulls away and gives me a quick kiss on the lips, making me want more. But he quickly becomes preoccupied with my wounds. I must look horrible. Dog bite, scratches on my face, not to mention the mud. I start to wipe my face with the edge of my shirt.

There's nothing worse than seeing your boyfriend after

so much time and looking like total crap. I probably smell too. Great.

Welcome back.

When Mo touches the bite, I wince. "It's not as bad as it could have been, considering the size of that hound."

I glance back at the dog that's lying still. He appears to be asleep, except for the smear of blood on one side. His silver tipped hair wiggles in the breeze.

A stab of regret pains me. "Why'd you have to kill him?"

Mo brushes my hair back and inspects the gash on my head. "Because he was going to kill you."

"You don't know that." I drop my head and say a quick Native American prayer. When I'm done, I sigh at the tragedy of it all.

"What would you have done if I hadn't shown up? You should have shot him."

"I don't know. I tried. I just couldn't." I don't mention the boy that killed or the girl that died. There's been too much death out here for me.

His moon-pie brown eyes find mine. He smirks and taps my nose with his finger. "Grace, it is one thing to love animals—help them and protect them. But if it's you or them, you only have a couple seconds to decide which one is more important."

"Maybe." I know Mo is right. But if I could save every animal, I would. Good or bad. Tame or wild. Dad always said, *they were here first.* "Poor Spike was probably trained to be mean so it wasn't his fault."

Mo squeezes my shoulder. "True. Let's get somewhere safe so we can take care of your arm. We don't want it getting infected." Practically the exact same thing I said to Dylan and Sadie.

My heart skips when he says "we. " Deep down, part of me is a bit miffed. Mo's been gone for a month and he says "we" as if we've never been apart. But the biggest part of me smiles that even after all the space and time between us, we are still a "we."

"Okay." I push to my feet and pat the dog's head as we pass by.

Mo picks up the gun and tucks it into his back pocket. Then he kneels by the man and rummages through his pockets until he finds an ID. "Gerald Brooks. Sound familiar?"

I shake my head. "No. But Uncle Bob has a whole crew with him, so I wouldn't know one bad guy from another."

The guy is still out cold as we walk across the grassy field through the rows of pine trees. I kinda wish Mo had killed the guy. Then I wouldn't have to worry about him tracking us. But Mo is like every good guy; he only kills if he absolutely has to.

The adrenaline begins to wear off and the pain stomps along my arm. I suck air through the space in my teeth when the throbbing worsens.

A loud banging noise makes Mo quicken his steps. He holds my elbow, forcing me to walk faster. "Let's hurry. We don't want to get caught out here by any of that Bob's blokes. They don't seem that friendly."

I watch him scan the horizon, making a plan. I can see he's making a plan because he gets a crease between his eyes when he gets intense. The way the light highlights his face makes me want to kiss him, pain or no pain. Mo appears much leaner than I remember, more fit. And his face appears tan, like he's been running outside.

I reach up and rub my hand over his short black hair. "When did you cut it?"

"When it got hot." He grabs my hand and holds it tight. "You like it?"

"I like you."

"I know."

I play-punch him in the arm. "You're bad, you know that."

"Bad huh?" He smirks his little lopsided grin and kisses the top of my hand. "Maybe I need you to keep me on the good side."

"Sounds a little Star Wars to me." He doesn't react, making me wonder if an English boy like him has ever even watched an American movie. I can't wait until the day when we can cook and sit around watching TV. Not have to worry about hiding or being apart. He grips my hand tighter and pulls me after him. His pace quickens, making me lag one step behind.

"How in the world did you find me out here?"

"I'm that good." He lifts his eyebrows. Then lowers them and frowns. "By the way, I thought I told you to lie low."

His comment catches me off guard. "I did. I have been."

"Imagine this." Mo keeps glancing over his shoulder, probably making sure no one follows. "I'm at my place, watching T.V., and flip to the news."

I stumble a few steps behind him. "Not much news in North Carolina since I left, huh?"

"Oh on the contrary. I stop and watch a cute little protest going on at some Florida roadside zoo." He eyes me over his shoulder. "Every mayor's daughter gets serious air time if she's a rebel. It's TV 101."

I cover my mouth. Uncle Bob already mentioned the protest. "Oh no. You mean it was in North Carolina too?"

"Affirmative. I'm watching and suddenly this beautiful girl walks up and stands her ground next to a protestor while some jerk's yelling in the background...by the way, you were the beautiful girl."

I grin. "Thank you." I rub my eyes. How is it I always make a bigger mess of things? "I'm so sorry. I didn't even think about it when I went to help. Had no clue about the publicity around it."

"Your erratic impulsiveness is one reason why I love you." He bends over and kisses my forehead. "But of course, I jumped in the car and drove straight down. Because if I saw it..."

"Maybe Al saw it too?"

He shrugs. "Not saying that, but I had to make sure you were safe. By the time I reached Birdee's, she was hysterical. Talking about you and Dylan disappearing along with the mayor's daughter."

I take a couple quick steps to catch up. "Is she okay? I mean, Birdee. I hope she wasn't that upset."

"Of course she was upset." Mo stops and faces me. "Why do you always worry about others when you should just worry about yourself? Trust me, you have enough on your hands with that."

I squint. "Very funny."

He stares at my lips for a second. "Gosh, I want to kiss you. But I need to get you safe first."

"Sounds promising."

He pulls me forward and keeps talking, "Of course when I heard you were missing, at first, we all assumed it was Al."

"We?"

"Your mom, Rex and me."

I feel sick again. "My poor mom. I bet she's a wreck."

"Do you blame her? She raced down as soon as she heard. Once we pieced it all together and tracked you to Uncle Bob's, it was obvious the kidnapping was unrelated to Al. I found some property papers that showed me Uncle Bob's property lines out here. I came out here and found some tracks. The rest was pure luck."

"Well, I'm glad you did."

For the next thirty minutes, Mo and I venture into the

thicker part of the woods where we can hide in bushes, trees, or under families of palms.

Once we're deep enough and sure we have no one tailing us, Mo finds a place tucked behind some bushes. "We'll stay here tonight. Tomorrow we have a long hike. If all goes well, we can have you home by nightfall."

"Home." I crawl in and lean against a log. "Sounds nice and clean." As he creates a make shift door for coverage, I take out a cloth and wipe my face and hands.

Once he's sure we're properly concealed, he faces me. "I should have done this when I first saw you, but I was preoccupied."

"With saving my life. How dare you?"

Mo leans in and gently kisses me as if he's unsure and it's our first time. Both of our eyes are open and locked in on the other. His lips feel velvety on mine. His kiss so soft, it's like a butterfly whisked by without me seeing. He pulls away and pushes a piece of hair off my face. "I missed you, Blossom."

I inch closer. "Yeah? I missed *that*."

"Oh, I got more where that came from." He puts his hand on my cheek and rubs his thumb along my jawline. Or is he wiping gunk off my face?

"I'm sorry. I probably look horrible."

"You look great to me."

Mo grabs my waist and pulls me closer. When we're only inches apart, he leans in, pressing his perfectly clean lips to my filthy ones. He holds my face so I can't pull away. His mouth is warm; I relax, settling in to him. Our lips move together sweetly like they always do. Mo has a way of making me forget the bad, forget the horror of the last few days.

When I sense him smiling, it forces me to grin too. His fingers try to rake through my knotted hair and then they dance softly down my spine. His hand rests on the small of my back and then presses me closer.

I obey and climb on his lap, wanting so much to disappear into him, blend my body with his. Hide. His lips become more urgent on mine, frantic almost. Like he's realized all he missed or all he lost. Not sure which one. Everything we haven't been able to say over the last few months is said in that one kiss.

We come up briefly for air and I take in his gorgeous face. The angles. The stubble. Those damn eyes. I think I'm going to die from happiness. Right here. Right now.

In the middle of this stinky swamp...in the middle of death and fear...

...Somehow, love and beauty manage to win.

Mo cups both hips, keeping me close to him. So no space or air can circulate between us. So nothing cools down the slow-burning heat we create together. His heart beats hard and fast against my chest, in rhythm with mine. The sparks are undeniable, almost addictive. They make me a bit dizzy, until everything around us disappears. We give in and let ourselves get lost in each other.

I pull away first, not to stop, but to breathe. A gentle breeze flutters over the invisible flame, extinguishing the smoldering heat. The kiss falls gently between us. Our breath comes out in short, desperate gasps and then slows. The intensity washes away and love settles in for the night.

I rest my forehead against his and open my eyes, waiting for the world to come back into focus. Suddenly, I realize I didn't give this guy enough credit.

A month away didn't change us at all.

It only made us stronger.

Mo gasps. "You are going to be the death of me, Grace Wells."

SURVIVAL SKILL #19

If you get dehydrated, rainwater and morning dew are both pure enough to drink straight from the source.

The sound of a screech owl pulls me out of my trance. The night comes in fast.

Mo glances up at the sky, now black painted with white dots. "We should get comfortable before night comes."

He gathers some palm and ferns for bedding and hands me a few branches to clean. I use my knife to strip off clumps of Spanish moss with the hopes of avoiding an invasion of the chiggers. I've learned that lesson the hard way. Not fun.

While Mo creates an awning of leaves to keep us hidden, I dig a hole for another fire. Even though it's muggy, a fire always lifts low spirits. Keeps the bugs away too. Out of the 5,008 mosquitoes, 5,001 have already bitten me by now.

Out here, they're relentless.

Starving, I scarf down a few of Mo's snacks. My belly hasn't been full in days. After food, Mo and I spend the night whispering and catching up on all little details we missed over the last month. I tell him about saving Cat. I tell him about the runaway girl they shot in the back and the ginormous liger out looking for a human meal. But I'm not ready to talk about the boy yet.

He finally asks me about Dylan and Sadie, which makes me go quiet.

Once I explain what happened, he strokes my hair. "I'm sure they're fine. Dylan is one tough bloke. Built like a house, I hear. I'm afraid of him and I don't even know him."

"You? No, impossible. You're not afraid of anything." I poke a stick at the fire and watch the embers dance into the air. They disappear in thin air before they can reach the palms above us.

"That's not true." Mo pokes the dimple in my chin. "I'm afraid of one thing."

"What?" I find his eyes, waiting for his answer. I can only assume he's going to say Al. I'd have to second the motion.

"Losing you."

"Well. That's not going to happen." I try not to smile too big. No matter how down or scared I get, Mo always lifts my spirits.

"I'm not going to lie. As long as Al's free, you'll always be in danger."

I nod as the urge to sob crams in my throat. "I know. But right now we need to focus on getting out of this place so we can send help to Dylan and Sadie. Then we can worry about Al."

Not that the worry ever goes away.

I haven't known Dylan or Sadie for very long, but I consider them good friends and can only hope they're both together and okay. I want so much to go after them; but right now, the best way to help is for me to return to civilization in one piece, and nab these men so they can't hurt anyone else. Then I can send out a rescue team.

Two deaths have already happened.

I pray Sadie and Dylan aren't added to that list.

Mo runs his hands over his head. "I'm always worried about Al, Grace. And about you."

I hug him as the fire crackles in front of us. "That's stressful, worrying about me all the time. You know, I can take care of myself."

"It worries me even more that you think that." He pulls my head onto his shoulder and kisses the top. "I hate to tell you this...but you have a stubbornness and impulse problem."

Dad used to say, *Grace, your head is harder than stone.*

This makes me smile. "Surprisingly, I've heard that somewhere before."

"I bet."

Mo and I snuggle in for the night. The backdrop sounds of the evening play a harmony to the buzz of our voices as we whisper.

My eyes flutter open and shut, listening to his voice. For the first time since I've been stuck out here, I finally feel safe. Like I can actually sleep. I spend the whole evening wrapped in Mo's arms, like a butterfly in a cocoon. With Mo around, transformation always happens.

I morph from being a scared and dirty Grace to a confident and beautiful one.

A change only he can inspire.

I close my eyes and listen to the crickets. I drift off thinking about home.

This time tomorrow I'll be back with Birdee and Mom, safe and clean once again.

At least, I hope.

Mo and I wake up and start hiking before the sun rises. I slept better than ever. Though by the looks of his bloodshot eyes—combined with the obsessive yawning and dark circles under his eyes—Mo stood guard all night.

The woods eventually blend into the musty swamps. The

heat, bugs, and wet are starting to get to me. The Everglades is a mosaic of different terrains, each holding its own set of dangers. The only thing that pushes me through my discomfort is the fact that we are close to home.

Mo and I move through the water-soaked swamp and into a muddy bog. A place where the Earth can literally swallow you whole. Never to be seen again. The swamp mud grows thick and goopy.

Each time I lift my feet out of mud to move forward, my muscles fatigue even more.

"This stuff is so thick, it's disgusting. Smells funky too."

"Just watch your step." Mo says from a few feet ahead.

I get a glimpse of a darker patch in front of him.

I yell out. "Mo, stop!"

He takes one more step and sinks up to his waist.

I freeze where I am and watch him dip a few more inches. He wiggles around, trying to get out, and drops further into the goopy hole. Brown mud bubbles up each time he drops an inch.

"Stop moving. It's a mud hole. The more you move, the more you'll sink."

He scoffs, obviously frustrated and weary. "Tell me something I don't know."

"Get your arms out so you don't sink lower."

He works to yank one arm free and then the other.

I search the area until I spot a stack of large sticks. "Wait."

"I'll try not to go anywhere." I know he's half kidding but I don't laugh. Rex told me about these holes when I first moved down here. They're hard to spot unless you know what to look for or you drop into one. And these spots can suck you down fast. Like thick quick sand. Rex said they could be big enough to swallow a whole truck. His friend got trapped in one, one time, while out jogging. Was stuck for three days. By the time they found him, he was barely alive, covered in bug bites, and delirious from drinking the swamp water.

Others have not been so lucky.

My heart races thinking of Mo drowning in that nasty hole.

I sift through the sticks, testing for the longest, strongest one. One that won't snap under Mo's weight.

I glance over my shoulder and watch Mo settle into the bog a few more inches. The mud is now up to his chest.

I try to sound calm. "Morris Cameron! I said stop moving. Jeez, talk about me being stubborn."

"It's like it's sucking me under," Mo says as he stops struggling. "I don't feel a bottom."

Because there is no bottom.

"Just hold on." I finally find a thick stick, about four-feet long and test its strength. It holds my weight without snapping in two, so I move as close as I can without stepping in the thickening mud.

"Hurry," is all Mo says. The frown lines across his forehead have deepened. Even though his face appears panicked, strained, his voice doesn't reflect that one bit.

I throw the stick to Mo, who is now submerged up to his chin. I want to run over and help. But if we both get stuck, we both die.

"Okay. Take the stick and put it across the mud in front of you. It'll help you get more surface area." He grabs it with both hands. "Now. Use it to try and work yourself out."

Mo shifts his lower body around. He lays his chest across the stick and rocks back and forth, trying to loosen his legs. I can hear the sucking sounds as the mud protests his escape.

"Keep going. It's not going to be easy."

As he shifts back and forth, mud splashes across his face, getting in his eyes, but he doesn't care. And he doesn't stop.

I stand on the side, helpless. With each minute, the urge to jump in and help grows stronger.

All I care about is saving my boyfriend from being eaten alive by a sinkhole.

When I can't take it any more, Mo finally gets his waist above the mud line. He grips the stick and rolls his feet out of the hole. Then he army crawls across the mud with the stick out in front of him. One move at a time. When he reaches me, I grab the belt loops on his pants and pull him up onto hard ground. Like trying to pull a cork out of a bottle.

Finally, he pops out.

Mo finally sits his butt up on the ledge and breathes heavy. He looks like a Sasquatch, brown from head to toe.

"You okay?" I ask.

He takes his dirty hand and wipes my cheek with the hopes of cleaning it. Instead, he muddies my face more. "Thanks to you. I have to admit I was a little scared there for a second."

"You? Never." I lean over and kiss his soiled lips. "I know you want to relax but we need to keep going."

"Yes we do."

Mo and I continue hiking through the swamp. The dirt path grows even hotter and stickier than ever. At first, the caked mud hanging on our clothes and skin keeps us cool. But once it dries in the heat, it becomes stiff and scratchy. The sun dims like a light being turned down and gray clouds roll in from the east. Lightning and thunder sound off in the distance.

"Please let the rain come and wash us off."

"Or we could rinse off in the water." Mo points to a swampy pond covered in floating algae.

I shake my head. "I prefer alligator-less swimming holes."

"They're actually pretty docile creatures unless..."

I take the corner of my shirt and wipe mud from my eyes. "...Unless you are a possible meal."

Speaking of food makes us hungry so we split one of Mo's high calorie bars and the last of the water before pushing on.

Eventually, the sky gives us a gift and dots the dry earth with refreshing rain.

I tip my head back and check out the gray sky. "Thank God."

I stand with my eyes closed, trying to wash the caked mud off my skin. My face. My clothes. Mo opens his mouth and takes a drink of water. We both relish in the coolness of the afternoon storm. The stale air fills with the nature's perfume of rain mixed with clean grass. I pull out my pony-tail holder and shake the dirt from my hair.

By now, I'm soaked to the bone, but at least I'm clean.

Mo takes off his shirt and wrings it out, pulling off clumps of mud. The rain trickles down his tan skin, making dark wet streaks. He busts me watching and covers his chest with his soaking shirt like he's modest.

"Oi! No peeking."

The heat and color of embarrassment crawls up my neck as I turn around. "Sorry. I forgot you were so English-proper."

A second later, he's behind me, whispering in my ear. "Well I am. Are you?"

I spin into him and wrap my arms around his waist. His skin is slick and warm. "You're a big tease."

"Who says I'm teasing?" He kisses me once. Twice. Three times before pointing at the path. "We better keep going. We're almost there."

"Too bad." A voice startles me from behind. "You two aren't going anywhere."

I recognize the voice.

Uncle Bob is back.

Before I can run into the swamps for cover, the liger guards my path. His tail flicks back and forth to a steady rhythm.

Even though I've seen the huge hybrid lion/tiger before, his enormous features, his undeniable beauty, and his very large fangs—all make me choke on my breath. This thing makes a panther look like a house mouse.

Mo – on the other hand – stares, eyes huge and round. This is his first encounter with Hercules, so the shock lingers.

He remembers to breathe and mumbles, "Blimey."

Mo and I slowly turn around and face Uncle Bob. He's leaning on a shotgun like he's got all day. Neither of us says a word.

"Fancy finding you here." Uncle Bob leans on the butt of his gun and smiles at me. Then he eyes Mo. "You're a bonus. But I wouldn't run if I were you. Hercules loves to play chase."

When we don't respond, he addresses me again. "I must say, Grace, I underestimated you. You've gotten further than anyone I've brought out here. I'm impressed."

"Am I supposed to say thanks?" My words are sharp, but they bounce right off Uncle Bob because he laughs.

I keep my wits in tune. Act tough. Don't cry. This is the only way to handle psycho guys like this. Show. No. Fear. They feed off control so if you don't give it to them, they start to unravel. I learned this information the hard way. If I pretend not to be scared, I may not live but at least I have a slim chance. It's like in the wild. If prey runs, it is hunted down and killed.

But, if the prey stays and fights, sometimes, and with a little help from Mother Nature herself, the predator will give up and go away.

Should I be so lucky?

I shove my hands in my pocket, making Bob flinch. I smile at gaining the small ounce of control. "You may have caught me. But my friends, Dylan and Sadie, are way ahead of me."

Uncle Bob laughs and takes off his hat to wipe his forehead. "Pretty sure that's a lie. We killed that boy two days ago."

His words force me to take a step back. "What?" I don't know whether I want to scream or cry.

Mo shakes his head and touches my shoulder. "Don't believe him. That's a lie."

Uncle Bob acts as though Mo said nothing. Instead he rattles my resolve with more information. "The girl got away. But don't worry, one of my boys is hot on her *tail*, Oh, I mean trail." He sneers at the stupid slip and spits tobacco on the ground. If this dude was five inches taller, a couple inches wider, and a few years younger, he could pass for Al.

"So who's your boyfriend?" He walks up to Mo and

inspects him. When Mo moves. Uncle Bob picks up his gun and puts it to Mo's forehead. "Someone you picked up in the woods?"

Mo pretends the gun isn't against his brain. He steps in front of me. "Actually, I'm part of the Fish and Wildlife Service. And I'm fairly positive this is all very illegal."

Uncle Bob keeps his gun on Mo. "Don't buy it son. You're too young to be any kind of officer. He frowns. "And you probably should know you picked the wrong company to keep. See, this girl is on my Most Wanted list. Unfortunately for her, she and her tree hugger friend stuck their noses up in my business. Trespassed on my property. B&E into my pens. And stole my animal. This girl can't be trusted. She has to pay."

"Not as long as I'm here," Mo says.

"I'll have to change that then." Uncle Bob cocks his gun.

Mo lunges at him and knocks him to the ground.

Uncle Bob yells, "Hercules, attack."

The liger lunges for me.

I duck, expecting a blow, but a rope that is tied around his neck catches on the tree, pulling him back. It takes my heart and me a second to absorb the scene.

I take a few steps back to make sure I'm out of reach. My body relaxes. "Oh I'm sorry, Uncle Bob. Hercules is a little tied up right now. Maybe you guys should let your animals roam free." The observation is a good one. If Hercules is such a great pet, why is he leashed all the time? Unless Bob is scared of his liger too.

Uncle Bob snarls like a cat and jumps to his feet. He throws a punch at Mo who's in a fighting stance, moving in a small circle.

Mo slides out of the way and then slams his double-fist down on Uncle Bob's back.

Uncle Bob grunts but only goes down on one knee. He

pulls a knife out of his back pocket and pops out the switch-blade. "Let's party, boy."

They both circle each other in a standoff. Only I've seen Mo fight. And he's only gotten better. I wouldn't want to get on his bad side.

When Uncle Bob moves closer to me, he reaches out and grabs my arm, putting the knife to my neck.

Mo stands upright and freezes. "Let her go."

"I'd rather not. Step back or I'll kill her." Uncle Bob's breath is hot on my ear and smells like beer and smoke mixed. The scent makes my stomach ripple.

Mo takes a step forward. "Don't hurt her."

"Oh! You care about this chick. So it's not just some Tarzan & Jane bootie call. Good to know." Uncle Bob presses the sharp blade against my skin. The steel feels as if it's burning my flesh.

The liger thrashes by the tree, clawing at his throat, desperate to escape his man-made leash.

The familiar scene brings me back to the first time I ran into Al and Billy in the woods. No telling what those two men would have done to me if Mo hadn't shown up in time. The fact that he had to save me then and thinks he needs to save me now bugs me. I need to depend on myself to get out of sticky situations that I put myself in.

It's what Dad taught me.

I've been through so much in the last year. Yet I've come through it and managed to survive. If I can outsmart Al, this short Everglades squatter isn't taking me down.

Without warning, I jam my elbow into Uncle Bob's gut. He goes a bit limp and coughs, long enough for me to turn around and knee him in the groin. The old timer drops like a bag of sand.

Uncle Bob forces himself to his feet and tries to cut

Hercules lose. "I'll let Hercules deal with you so I can take on your pathetic boyfriend."

I let my hands hang, nice and relaxed, preparing for any attack. From any side. "Why are you doing this? You know it's not going to end well. It can't."

"Simple. I'm bored." Uncle Bob continues releasing the liger. "I've been hunting my whole life. You name it, I've killed it. Moose, bears, lions. Even elephants. The wildest in the world. There's nothing else to hunt."

I make a face at the thought of him preying on animals as well as people. "So what? Now you kidnap runaways?"

I can feel Mo's presence behind me, but he doesn't move. He's waiting for something. I can feel it. The moment will come.

"Kidnap? No, they come willingly. I offer them everything they don't have. Money, food, shelter. Most of them don't want to end up on the streets. That girl you saw didn't ask one question. The boy was a bit more trouble, but he cooperated in the end. To be fair, he almost lasted as long as you."

"You're sick."

He shifts his knife into the other hand. "You have no idea. Go get her Hercules." The rope snaps, freeing the beast. Only instead of charging me, Hercules jumps on Uncle Bob's back.

Uncle Bob screams the liger's name and tosses out commands. "Hercules, heel!" He reaches for his belt but the whip isn't there.

The liger doesn't listen or obey. Instead, he lets go for a split second and regrips Uncle Bob by his throat, pinning him down.

Mo pulls me behind him. "Don't move."

I grip his waist and bury my head in his shirt. I can't watch.

A scream from Uncle Bob is followed by some gurgling sounds and crunching noises.

I cover both ears.

See no evil, hear no evil.

Blocking out the world, I admit that deep down part of me wants to help this man. Save him from a grisly death. But I can't take on a crazed semi-truck-of-an-animal for some lowlife who killed an innocent girl, who tried to kill me, and who probably murdered my friends too.

The large cat doesn't move until Uncle Bob finally stops thrashing.

It feels like it takes forever. The seconds stretch into minutes, which feel like hours.

Until it's finally over.

Uncle Bob is dead.

Hercules lies down next to his kill and licks Uncle Bob's bloody face.

Mo and I have slowly backed into a bush but are still in the animal's view if he turns.

"I can't believe he killed his owner," I whisper.

"He doesn't know," Mo says quietly. "He's wild. It's ingrained in him to hunt. They always go for the easiest and closest kill."

Hercules' ear locates us behind the bush, but he does nothing. His ears lie back against his head, eavesdropping on our conversation. He licks his massive paw, which is at least the size of my whole head.

Mo's right.

Wild animals are meant to be wild. No matter what. You can't tame them. Mother Nature sees to that. She gives them what they need. No human can take that away.

Mo raises his gun and aims at Hercules.

When he's about to pull the trigger, I push his hand out of the way. "Don't."

"That thing will eat us if he gets the chance." Mo keeps his hand on the trigger but lowers his arm.

"He's not attacking us now." I say quietly. "We can't just kill to kill."

Mo stays alert and kisses my head. "That's why I love you. You actually believe in something and try to do something about it. Not many people do that. Especially if their life is threatened."

I smile and squeeze him from behind.

Hercules stands, putting Mo on Defcon four. If the liger walks this way, he's dead. Instead of attacking, the liger picks up his owner by the shoulder and drags him into the thickest part of the woods. Not a moment of remorse or thought.

Nothing wasted.

Animals kill to eat. Not for fun.

"See? He didn't want us. He got his meat and now he's gone."

Mo puts the gun away. "At some point, you may have to kill an animal if it's attacking you. What are you going to do then?"

"I'll know when the time comes."

Mo leans against a rock and watches the spot where Hercules disappeared. "It's not bad, you know."

"What isn't?"

He grabs my belt loop and pulls me close. "It's not bad to kill an animal in defense. Or if you're hunting for food. It's the way people abuse and slaughter animals—for fun—that's what is so bad."

"Why are you telling me this?" I shrug and try to wiggle out of his iron embrace. Mo always does this tough hug when he wants me to listen. Because he can say what he wants and I can't get away.

"I want to make sure you aren't forgetting the difference. Or it could cost you."

I frown and turn my head when he goes to kiss me. "I don't need a lecture on animal conservation."

"I'm not lecturing, Grace. I'm keeping you safe." He smirks and tightens his hold like a boa constrictor on a rabbit. No squirming. No getting away. "You may need to make a decision in a split second out in the wild and if you ever hesitate...you could die."

"I won't. But thank you for the PSA." I rub his face with the back of my hand. His stubbles scratch my flesh, but I don't care.

Mo and I kiss for a second.

"I need you to stay safe."

"I'm safer when you're around. Besides, I'm strong. All on my own."

"I hope so. Not sure I could live with myself if anything happened to you." He tips his head back and studies the sky. We're both still damp from the light shower but somewhere in the last ten minutes, it stopped.

To leave, we have to walk past the place where Uncle Bob was attacked by his own pet.

Blood smears mark the ground in the direction Hercules dragged the body.

I stop and stare, feeling numb. Something changes in me in that moment. I don't feel sick. Don't feel scared. In fact, I don't feel anything. A year ago, this bloody scene would have bothered me. Now, it doesn't penetrate my wall. Now, it doesn't matter to me.

"You okay?" Mo asks.

I nod, but sadness simmers in my gut, causing my throat to clench.

I'm not sad because Uncle Bob died.

I'm sad because this is the first time I don't care.

Death doesn't bother me as much as it used to.

And I'm not sure that's a good thing.

SURVIVAL SKILL #21

When hiking, know where you are going. Study a map of the area and make sure to bring it with you—being able to pinpoint your location will increase your chances of being found.

I'm so tired that my body sleeps as I walk.

My limbs are heavy. My body aches. But my brain refuses to give in to the exhaustion.

I have to make it home. If it's the last thing I do.

We are out of food, out of water, and out of time.

Hours later, I finally spot Birdee's fence at the edge of the Everglades.

My body recharges, waking up, and I get a third wind. I quickly kiss Mo on the cheek and run ahead. I can hear him jog behind me. Staying close enough, but not too close to stop me from racing to my freedom.

I made it.

"Birdee! Birdee!" I scream her name as I'm running through the sharp saw grass. The emotions that have been trapped deep inside me for the last few days bubble over. "Birdee! Birdee!"

My grandmother opens the screen door and looks around in disbelief, as if she's not sure of the source.

"Birdee!" Tears stream down my face as I climb her fence and fall onto her lawn.

"Chicken!" When she spots me, she races toward me with her arms outstretched. I don't slow down until I slam into her, taking her down to the ground with me. She doesn't care about the crash. Her arms fold around me like a bat's wings.

I am home.

"Oh, Chicken." She pecks my head with kisses. Then she yells, "Mary! She's back!" Birdee hugs me hard one more time then pushes me away. She scans my body for wounds, scratches—anything she can fix or bandage. She touches the bandaged bite on my arm and the gash on my head. Then she hammers me with questions. "Are you okay? Where have you been? Are you hurt?"

Mo jumps the fence and walks up.

Birdee releases her death grip and holds up her hand. He helps her to her feet and she bear hugs him. Almost harder than she squeezed me. "Thank you, boy. I owe you everything."

"You owe me nothing, Miss Birdee." Mo leans down a few inches and hugs her.

Over her shoulder, I see Mom burst through the door and stomp down the porch steps.

Even though every muscle screams, I jump up and practically trip across the lawn to get to her.

She stops running when she's only a few feet away, as if pretending to be calm, and then races over and clutches onto me.

She doesn't say a word. The lines etched in her forehead hint that she wants to yell but is so thankful she can't complain. I feel guilty for causing her so much worry over the last year since Dad died. Mom deserves a break from all this horror. Neither of us has gotten one yet.

Rex shows up and lifts his baseball hat slightly to mimic a polite hello. "Hallo, mooi een!" His grin fades as he glances over my shoulder at Mo. His eyes dart past both of us and scan the bushes beyond the border of the yard. As if waiting for someone to come.

"Rex—" I whisper.

"—Grace? Where's Dylan?" Rex crumples his hat in his hands. "Where's Sadie?"

I pull away from Mom. "We were hoping they already made it back?" This was probably just dumb hope but part of me believed Dylan and Sadie would simply hike in and wait for us. I banked on the fact that Uncle Bob was bluffing about hurting either of them. I convinced myself he lied.

"No. They're not here. I was hoping they would come back with you. That Mo would have found them too."

"I never saw either one," Mo says weakly.

Birdee walks over to Rex and drapes her arm around him. She tries to sound extra peppy. "Hon, I'm sure they're right behind them. Right, Chicken?"

I want to burst into tears. Cry. Scream. Because I'm not so sure they're ever coming back. Alive. I can't speak words so I nod instead.

"Grace?" Mom reaches over and squeezes my shoulder. "Can you tell us happened out there?"

I avoid Rex's eyes and try not to sound as worried as he looks. "When I went to find Cat, the panther, Sadie and Dylan came looking for me. But Uncle Bob showed up and grabbed me. He must have had serious help because when I came to, we were all together. He and his creepy buddies had taken us far out in Everglades. They killed that runaway girl in front of us..."

"The one on T.V.?" Birdee asks.

When I nod, Mom gasps and presses her hand against her heart. "Oh my goodness, that poor girl."

Birdee throws her straw hat on the ground. "Bunch of crazy men!"

"Birdee!" Mom yells and then lowers her voice. "Go on."

Words spill out of my mouth like water pouring out of a full pitcher. "They made us run. Tried to hunt us down, but we separated." The more I talk, the more out of breath I get. Images flash in my mind as I spit out a quick rendition of all that happened. "Sadie and Dylan found me eventually but the men, they were coming after us. Dylan distracted them while we got away."

"So where's Sadie?"

I clear my throat. "She wanted to go back for him."

"And you let her?"

The voice is unfamiliar, so I raise my head. Behind Rex is a woman that resembles Sadie. Same disheveled dark hair. Same bright eyes. Same thin frame. Her face is puffy and streaked and her fancy mayor's wife's suit is dirty and wrinkled. "You left my Sadie out there? Alone?"

I can only stare, not knowing what to say.

Mo comes next to me. "Grace wanted to go after Sadie. But I wouldn't let her go back. It was too dangerous."

I glance at his talking. I left Sadie. And it had nothing to do with Mo. Mo came later. He's taking the blame for me.

The woman crosses her arms in anger but her expressions are conflicted. Her furrowed eyebrows tell me she is mad but her frown and tears remind me she is heartbroken. "You let Sadie stay out there. When it was that bad? Why? Why wouldn't you bring them both back home? Why just her?"

Mom obviously senses the mounting tension. She kisses me on the head and beelines to the woman's side. She grabs both of her hands. "Cammie, I'm sure Sadie and Dylan are together. Let's go inside and call the police. Give them an update. They'll help us find them. Both." She cups Cammie's elbow and leads her back into the house. I hear the woman sobbing as the door slams behind her.

I'm left outside with Rex, Birdee and Mo.

Rex sighs, his lip quivers and his hands are pinned on his hips. He straddles the line between breaking down and being strong. "Any idea where they went?"

"I can show you where I was on a map. That is a starting place."

"Good. That's a start." Rex walks to his car and pulls out a map of the Glades.

"I'm going to call Sweeney." Mo squeezes my hand. "He'll send extra help."

Birdee overhears and butts in. "I'm not sure we need Sweeney around. Do we? He's nothing but trouble as far as I'm concerned." When she sees Rex's face, her shoulders sag and her stubbornness crumbles. "But...if anyone can help, it's him."

Rex spreads out the map as I point out the last location where I saw Sadie and Dylan. He marks the spots with a pen and folds it back up. "Let's hope Uncle Bob doesn't find them first."

"He won't." I spout out and look at Mo, hoping he'll fill in the gaps.

Mo steps up like he always does. Anything to take care of me in any way. "His pet liger killed him. Grace and I watched the whole thing."

Birdee cups her mouth. "That's a horrific way to go, but I can't say I'm not glad."

"Serves him right." Rex says.

She touches his arm. "See hon, we'll find them. Hope is not dead until we kill it."

"I'm going to get started." Rex leaves us and climbs in his truck.

Birdee tries to grab my arm to stop me from chasing him, but I run over to his window. Rex sits with both hands on the steering wheel with his head bowed forward.

"I'm sorry. He'll be okay. You'll see." I cup his hand and try to give him some comfort, though I'm not sure I believe what I'm saying. I want to believe it but that doesn't make it true. "Dylan is the strongest man I know."

"I hope you're right, Grace." Rex starts the car as I take a few steps back. "Because if he's not, I lose the only son I ever had. I'm not sure me or my family will ever be okay again."

As Rex backs down the driveway, Mo and Birdee head inside.

I stay out until Rex drives away.

I feel his pain. The day Dad died, a part of me died with him.

I pray today is different.

That whole night I toss and turn.

I can't stop thinking of Dylan and Sadie. Of the liger hunting us down. And of the men who started this whole sick game.

How many other kids did Uncle Bob hunt? How many animals did he kill? And what about all the animals at his house? Who's been feeding them the last few days?

Finally at about five in the morning, I go ahead and get dressed.

I head downstairs into the living room.

Mo is fast asleep on the couch. He's lying on his back with a blanket pulled up to his waist. No shirt on. I resist peeking under the covers. Boxers or briefs? I can only assume he's wearing something. Faint tan lines draw perfect lines along his waist. His hair is messy and he has one arm draped over his face, as if he's blocking out any sliver of light. I can tell his face is newly shaven. He breathes heavy but not loud and obnoxious like a bear. It's actually comforting.

How can he sleep this hard? After all that's happened?

I sit in the chair across from him and watch him. I love how his long black lashes lie on his cheek. The way his lips part slightly to allow the lucky air in and out. How his chest moves up and down in a steady rhythm. When Mo is smooth-faced and asleep, he looks younger than the gruff unshaven guy from the woods. Yet even at 17 going on 18, he seems wiser than his years.

I love this guy.

Everything about him.

Sometimes I wonder why a calm and cool guy from across the pond—not to mention with a sexy accent—puts up with a back woods girl like me dressed in a heavy southern twang and who has a built-in impulse button that sits on top of the chip on my shoulder. Sometimes, most times, I feel broken. Cracked. But when Mo is around—when he looks at me—I grow stronger, like I could actually piece myself back together again.

Even after going through all the horror of the past few days, I still love that the minute he saw me on T.V.—thinking I was in trouble—he raced down here to make sure Birdee and I were okay.

Mo's not undependable like other guys my age. He's always here for me. He never hesitates to show me how he feels. Never plays games. And always ensures I'm safe and sound.

So why I am so scared of losing him all the time? Don't I deserve everything he gives me?

Or do I?

I move and sit on the ground next to him, lightly touching his black hair with my fingers. His breath still has the slight smell of mouthwash and his skin smells like Birdee's Dove soap.

No matter what's happened, somehow when I'm down and out, this guy makes me happy.

I lean over gently and brush my lips across his. It takes everything I have to hold back from jumping on top of him and giving him the real kiss he deserves.

The one I always think about. Want. Need. Love.

Petey flies over me and squawks, "Wake up!"

Mo jerks up and our heads bump, causing me to bite my lip. "Ouch."

"Blossom, I'm sorry." Mo says, rubbing his head.

I touch my lip to see if it's bleeding. Then I throw a magazine at Petey bobbing up and down on his perch. "Stupid bird."

Mo stretches and yawns then he puts both hands behind his head. "Miss Grace, were you trying to take advantage of me? Undressing me with those gorgeous green eyes?"

"No." I say. Then I can't help but smile. "I mean yes, kinda."

He pulls me on top of him. "Good. I like to be girl-handled. Only by my girl, of course."

I pop him in the forehead as my body tingles from being this close to him. "You better."

He reaches up and sweeps a piece of hair out of my face. "Trust me, I need no other."

Then Mo lifts his head and kisses me. It's perfect, as always. The light touch. The way he moves his lips over mine. The way he stops and kisses the sides of my lips before kissing me hard again. Everything about him is perfect. For me.

Amid all the love he gives freely, something inside me shifts every time we kiss. Something that will never be reversed. Each time, I open up a little. Mo saves me from shutting down completely. Without him, I would have sunk a long time ago.

I can dwell more on this feeling later; for now, I'm happy to feel his breath come and go in time to mine. I'm happy to relish his kiss: hard, but soft; fiery but cool— a split second in time, but it changes me forever.

So much is said in these kisses.

Petey squawks from where he perches at the window, "Here, kitty, kitty, kitty."

My eyes pop open and I jerk away. "Cat." How could I forget? In all this craziness, I've completely forgotten about the poor panther I was rescuing when Uncle Bob dragged me out into the swamps. I try to think back to when I last saw her. I remember taking off the rope, and her running away when I was hit from the back.

"Wait." Mo still has his eyes closed. "Stay with me for little longer."

I push off his chest and stand. "I can't."

"Bugger. I knew you'd say that." Mo pushes up and pulls on his shirt. "What is it? I can hear your wheels cranking out some crazy from here."

"I have to go." I rush over and yank on my hiking shoes.

Mo sits up and pulls on his shirt, arms first, then head. He rushes to the doorway right when I reach the threshold and stops me. "You—my dear—are not going anywhere. And I mean that in the least controlling way."

I grab my bag off the rack and check to make sure it has everything I need. Which reminds me of giving stuff to Sadie. Which reminds me my friend isn't here. She would want me to go find Cat. "I have to go to Uncle Bob's."

"Uh, negative," Mo says matter-of-factly. "Not a good plan."

When I try to move around him, he blocks my path. "I have to find Cat. The panther I told you about."

"No you don't."

"Why not? I say, crossing my arms in frustration.

"It's too dangerous."

I shake my head. "Uncle Bob is dead. We saw him die.

Unless we are afraid of zombies now, I'm pretty sure I'm safe at his place."

Mo's face changes as if he forgot that little fact. "We need to stay here until we figure this thing out. Sweeney should be here within the hour. He jumped in the car after I called him. We can go then. With back up."

"It won't take long. I need to find that panther. Then we can come back." I try to get past him again. "Mo, I'm serious. If Uncle Bob is dead, there are about fifty wild animals trapped in horrible cages and conditions, that haven't eaten in days. I need to go there and make sure Cat and the rest of them are okay."

"Sweeney will know what to do when he gets here."

"I don't want to go—" I raise my voice at first and then lower it so Birdee and Mom don't hear. "—I don't want to wait for Sweeney. It might be too late."

"You never do."

I move closer to him. "Please come with me. See if Cat is there. We can wait for Sweeney to help rescue the other animals if you want. Please." I rise up on my tiptoes and kiss him.

"If you are trying to manipulate me..." He grips my waist. "It's working." He leans down to kiss me again.

I grin and turn my head. "Come with me. We can have him meet us there."

He doesn't say anything.

I wait while he stares down at me. "Please? What's going to happen?"

He cups his hand over my mouth. "Don't say that. Every time you say that, something does."

"Mo, we saw Uncle Bob die. Hercules practically fed on him in front of us. No one's there. Except for the abused and starving animals."

"What about those other men? What if they show up?"

I tilt my head and narrow my eyes. He's trying to stall me, maybe hoping Birdee and Mom will get up. He knows they'll never let me leave now. To go anywhere. Ever again. "You know as well as I do those men aren't going to show up there. They probably know I've made it home by now and are hightailing their butts out of the state before the Feds can track them down." I kiss him again. "Did I mention that Cat is on the national endangered list? We can't afford to lose even one panther."

"Man, that is lower than low." Mo holds up one finger and leaves his guard post to put on his shoes. "I'll do this with you on one condition. You let me lead. And you listen to what I say. The whole time. I mean it."

"Wow. You drive a hard bargain."

He doesn't budge. "You want to go, don't you?"

Upstairs, I hear light footsteps walking around. Then a flush from the bathroom.

Someone's up.

If either Mom or Birdee comes down, there's no way I'm going anywhere. Especially not to Bob's place.

"Better make up your mind." Mo smiles wide and leans against the door. "Time's ticking."

"Fine. But we go now."

Mo opens the door and stops me from leaving first. "Remember, after me."

On the way to Uncle Bob's, the hot wind whips through my hair. I close my eyes and tilt my head toward the open roof, letting the sun warm my face.

Mo grabs my hand, but his eyes remain glued to the road. I can tell he's not happy about this plan.

For a second, I put aside everything that's happened over the last few days.

I try to forget that Sadie and Dylan are still missing. I try to forget that Uncle Bob almost killed me. And I try to forget that poor Annie was shot in the back and left as lunch.

For just one second, I pretend Mo and I are driving down to the beach. Al is long gone. I am safe. And we're going to spend the entire afternoon lying on the sand, eating a picnic, and kissing.

There must be kissing.

When the Jeep parks, I keep my eyes closed for one more second, reveling in my pretend world.

"You with me?"

I open my eyes and turn my head. "Always."

He hops out and comes around to open my car door.

Chivalry is not dead. Not as long as Mo is in this world.

I slide out of the car and follow Mo up to the fence.

Uncle Bob's place is dark and deserted. The first time I was here, it seemed less...run down. I didn't remember it being this depressing. A shiver runs down my spine, thinking of all those animals penned in the back. Though the place looks the same, I am different. It's scary how things—people—can change so fast. Even when you expect things to change, you are never prepared for how they will or when.

Faint growls and snarls drift from behind the building.

It tells me one thing: some animals are still alive. There's hope yet.

Sadie will be so happy.

I move over to the gate and shake it but it's draped with a heavy iron chain and lock.

"I'll have to climb over."

"Wait. I may have some bolt cutters."

I check Mo's face to see if he's kidding, but he's serious. "Because everyone carries those."

"I—Blossom—am not everyone." Mo leans over and kisses my nose. "Wait here."

I peer through the fence and holler through the slots, "Cat? Cat!" I follow up the calls with clicking noises. Pretty sure it won't work because it's not like the panther knows the nickname I awarded her.

A few minutes later Mo comes back. "No bolt cutters. But I have this." He raises a gun. "Stand back." Then he shoots off the lock.

I plug my ears and watch the chain clatter to the ground. "A little drastic, don't you think?"

Mo clicks the safety back on and sticks the gun in the back of his pants. "You want to get in, don't you?"

"Yes, but you'll scare the animals." I push open the gate. "Not to mention, this is illegal."

"Let me handle that."

Mo and I move toward the back pens when his phone rings. The noise is loud and startles me, sending my heart blasting out of my body.

"It's Sweeney." He holds his cell phone up in the air and swings around. "Can't get a bloody signal. Let me take this and I'll be right behind you. I'll get him to meet us here."

"Okay. Tell him that there are definitely a few animals alive so he may need help."

"Let's hope it's more than a few." Mo runs back up to his car on the dirt road and plugs his ear as he talks. He looks in my direction and covers his mouthpiece with one hand. "If you're scared, wait for me."

I scoff under my breath and yell back. "Yeah right. You wish!"

I walk around the side of the house where just days ago, Sadie, Dylan, and I were trying to rescue Cat ourselves. If I could rewind my life, I'd go back to that moment and make a hard decision to leave Cat behind, knowing it would save my friends. It's my fault they're missing. If I'd stayed at home that day, we'd all be safe now.

Then again, Cat would definitely have been dead. A necessary sacrifice?

That's the hard part for me. In the moment, when I make a decision, it feels like I'm doing the right thing. But in hindsight, I wonder if I would always make a different choice. Knowing the aftermath that follows.

A horrible smell finds my nose.

I smack one hand over may face and almost gag. The stench is so strong, it forces me to take a step back.

I know this smell.

The smell of death.

Bad memories of finding Simon mutilated in the Smokies back home flood back to me. Poor, sweet Simon. I wish I could have saved him. Sometimes, when I lie in bed, I wonder if Lucky, the little cub I did save, ended up making it on his own. I'd like to think he romps through the forest with his family and friends. But after knowing and experiencing the poaching problem first hand, I'm not sure that's possible.

I wave both hands over my head to try and capture Mo's attention, but his back's toward me.

I cover my mouth and nose with my shirt and force myself forward. I stop when I reach the first cage. One lion lies in the corner, covered in flies. I'm too late. Their condition was already bad enough; add a few days of not eating to it and it's hard to live on. Especially when there is nothing to live for.

My heart sinks as I approach the animals' prison to get a better view. The other lion lies behind the fake rock. I stop, expecting it to attack the cage again.

He forces himself to his feet and tries to make it across the floor. He's so skinny his rib bones are practically sticking out of his skin. He stumbles toward me and falls on the floor. He gives up and stays where he is. But he keeps his eyes on me.

Tears spring to my eyes.

Because his fight is gone.

This lion is giving up.

Which makes me want to save this place even more.

"It's okay boy I won't let you die." The lion sighs and drops his head to the cement. "I actually hope you want to eat me again someday."

I stand on my tiptoes and peek over to the next cage where Cat used to rest. Can't tell if it's empty or not. I hope I'm ready for what I may find.

I cautiously walk around the front of the lion cage and pinch my nose. The smell isn't only coming from the lion cage. It's everywhere. My heart races as I move closer and closer to the monkey cage. The last time I was here, these things were the loudest animals in here.

Now it's quiet.

Death has no voice.

I approach the cage. One monkey stands on top of a makeshift cardboard box.

I'm relieved. "Hey you. What? You got nothing to say today?"

The monkey picks up her dead baby and drags it behind her. When she reaches me, she drops the skin and bones at my feet. She nudges it and makes a few noises. As if she's talking. This needs no words. Then the mommy monkey sits and stares, as if waiting for me to make everything in her life okay.

I can almost hear her saying, *please help my baby.*

I squat down to her level and blink back tears. More dead monkey carcasses are in the back. The monkey must have moved them. Cleaned her space of death so hope could continue to live.

This is the problem with zoos like this one. Not only are these animals cared for improperly, but there are so many of them that only a few get any attention. Not love, not food, not anything they need or deserve. "I'm so sorry."

The mommy comes over and sticks her hand through the fence.

I reach into my backpack and pull out a box of raisins. I pour some in through the chain link and watch as she scarfs down every last one. Then she sticks her hand out again.

I don't have the heart to ignore her. She's already lost everything. I hand her the box. She snatches it and hobbles to the back corner with half the speed she once had. There, she eats, protecting her stash from all the other dead monkeys. She either doesn't know they're all gone or she's pretending not to know. We do what we have to do to survive.

I check to see if Mo's coming, but he's out of sight.

I swallow the lump in my throat and move onward, toward Cat's cage.

I pray with each step.

Please don't let Cat be there. Please don't let Cat be there.

I don't know why I need to save this panther. Or why I am so attached to something that will never, ever be mine. Maybe I just need to know I can make a difference. That I can save one. It won't make up for all the animals that died here or the ones that have died on my watch.

But it would make a huge difference to me.

I need to believe I can do something right in this world. I can make a difference.

When I stand in front of the cage, my eyes scan the large space. I open the door, which scrapes across the ground. Then I check behind the rock and in the very back.

The cage is empty. My body sags in relief. This doesn't mean Cat's alive, but it does mean she didn't die here. In the Everglades, she is free. Hopefully she gets a fighting chance.

It's time to go home and be with my family.

Someone whistles behind me.

"Mo, she's not here." I spin around but don't find anyone. "Mo?"

The whistling gets louder until I can make out the song. The tune slams into my memory bank.

Dixie.

Only one person I know whistled that haunting song.

Al.

I race to the cage door when Al steps out of the shadows. His eyes are narrow and his lips are plastered in a perma-sneer. "Well, well, well...long time, no see, Grace."

I come to a skidding stop and back up even quicker.

"No." My brain turns to mushy stuff and I can't think of another word to use.

In my head, I'm screaming them. But nothing comes out of my mouth.

For a moment, I freeze in time. For a moment, I'm not sure what I can do.

Al walks toward me. Slowly. Methodically.

He's still tall, bigger than I remember, and still very scary.

He pulls the cage door behind me, blocking us both inside. "We have some catching up to do."

Reason with the attacker. Fighting an individual should only be considered a last-resort method.

I move further back into the cage as he moves toward me. Finally, my back presses against the chain link.

My hand feels around, searching for the hole I cut away for Cat to escape. Then I try to squeeze through it.

Al grabs my arm.

I finally find my voice and scream. "Mo!"

My body freaks out as he wrestles me around the cage. I jerk free and spin around, punching him the face. He lets go and grabs his nose as I sneak past him.

"You little..." Al lunges after me and grabs my hair, dragging me out of the cage and along the uneven ground. My legs bump into rocks and scrape in the dirt.

Mo yells in the background. "Grace! Where are you?"

"Here!"

Mo comes sliding around the side of the house. Gun in hand. He freezes and his face drops when he sees Al. I spot a flash of something cross his face. Something I don't see on him often.

Fear.

This makes me freak out.

Al rolls me into his clutches and presses the large knife against my throat. "Boy, you shouldn't play with your daddy's guns."

Mo does look a bit strange. A 17-year-old pointing a big gun at a grown man. Only Mo's dead serious. He may be interning with Sweeney, but he also started the training. He's a natural, and better than Al knows or gives him credit for. Mo has lost everything. He has nothing else to lose.

But me.

I whimper a little as Al presses the blade closer. It nicks my skin and warm blood drips onto my shirt. I'm going to pass out. Seeing blood is one thing, seeing my blood is something else.

"Grace?" When I meet his eyes, the look I saw pass over him is gone. Nothing but confidence. Reassurance. "It's okay. I got this. Okay? Trust me."

Al laughs and jerks me around. "You ain't got nothing, boy. I've been waiting for this day for a long time. I ain't gonna give up so easily this time. Now, drop your weapon and back up. Or I swear to God I'll gut her this time. I won't make the same mistake twice."

Mo slowly lays down his weapon and reverses a few steps with both hands up. "Don't you hurt her. I swear to God—"

"You are no position to tell me what to do. You've had nine months to find me and yet, nothing. So this is on you and your old buddy Sweeney."

He pulls me toward Mo and keeps his vise grip around my neck and body. Like a boa constrictor on its prey, he doesn't relax the slightest bit.

But if he does, I'm ready.

"Please let me go."

"You don't want her Al. She's not worth your time. You want me—I'm the one that betrayed you. Broke your trust. I'm the one who rescued her father."

Al breathes heavy in my ear. "No. You did piss me off. But this girl has taken too much from me. Caused me a lot of hassle. My business, my sister. Been eating damn beans for a year."

"You brought all that on yourself," Mo says.

Al growls. "She's cost me a lot of money. She cost me a lot of heartache. Since day one."

The whole time they talk, Dad's face flashes through my mind. Al almost killed me once before. If it hadn't been for Dad blocking Al's bullet with his body, he'd still be alive today.

Dad died for me and I'm not going to let some dumb redneck get away with it.

I shift slightly to re-center my weight, but Al grips my neck tighter. He moves his lips against my ear. "Don't even think about it, sweetheart."

I relax and let him push open the cage door and drag me around the side of the house. This is not the time to fight. I'll get my chance.

Mo walks behind us with his hands up. He's not about to let me out of his sight. He tries to reason with Al the whole way. "Al, this will go a whole lot easier if you let her go."

My feet drag along the ground. I make myself extra heavy, making Al's movement harder.

He jerks me from side to side as he walks. One hand around my waist, the other hand still at my throat. "Already got a mountain load of charges. What's one more?" He stops at the broken down porch and waves the knife at Mo. "Stop right there."

Mo freezes. "What are you going to do, Al? There's nowhere to go. Sweeney and his men will show up in five minutes. If you go inside, you'll be trapped."

Al drags me up the stairs, still pressing the sharp blade against my throat. It feels like hot steel against my skin. I'm almost afraid to swallow. This isn't your average steak knife. This is a special hunting knife meant for serious damage.

I should know; I sold it to Al at Tommy's place last year. Before everything happened.

Al stops and makes me open the door. He pauses and studies Mo. "If anyone comes inside—or even close to this house—I'll gut her like a fish. You hear me? Her death will be on you."

Mo grips my eyes with his.

He says everything in that one look.

I love you. Trust me. You will be okay.

My face says something very different. Something I'm afraid to say out loud. Something I'm scared to even contemplate.

My look says, *goodbye.*

I keep my eyes on Mo until Al slams the door behind us. He throws me down on the couch and bolts the door.

I sit up and look around. Uncle Bob was a potential guest on the Hoarder show. Boxes of crap are stacked from floor to ceiling. Narrow paths create tunnels through the house. The guy obviously was a nut. Good riddance.

Without turning around, Al says, "Move and I'll kill yah."

And I believe him.

I remain still as he hangs blankets over the windows and pulls furniture in front of the doors. He makes sure we are barricaded in the living room with no way for anyone to see inside. Let alone bust through. The mounds of trash don't provide any escape routes either.

This man is not going down without a fight.

And unfortunately, I'm in the center of it with ringside seats.

I look at the ceiling, trying to take in a breath. Being used to the open space and fresh outdoor air makes it much harder to function in small, cramped spaces.

Breathe in. Out. In. Out.

Al fights his way into the kitchen. I hear the fridge door open. Shortly after, he returns with a beer and sits in the chair across from me. He pops off the top and takes a long drink.

"What are you going to do?"

He waves me off, frowning. "Let me think. I wasn't expecting your boyfriend to show up."

I try not to smile at Mo messing up Al's plans, but I keep my reaction buried. "You can't keep me here forever. How will you get out?"

Al stands and paces the room like the lions used to in their cage. He walks over to the front window and pulls back a sheet.

I lean forward and peek out.

A couple of black cars are outside, parked next to Mo's Jeep.

The cavalry has arrived. Thank God. Now I need to keep Al calm until I can come up with a plan to escape this rat hole.

"Al, if you let me go. I promise I'll distract them enough so you can get away."

He scoffs. "Yeah right. Like you did for Katie?"

My hands tremble. He knows. I figured he might, but I'm not sure how much he knows. Sweeney did such a good job hiding some details of that night in the snow. The scene creeps back into my memory. I remember hearing the gunshot and thinking it was Birdee. Thank God it wasn't. Katie took a shortcut.

The easy way out.

"I didn't hurt her. She hurt herself." Even though it's

true, Birdee and I still feel guilty. Especially Birdee since she was the one who watched Katie kill herself. The lady would have rather died than face the media in cuffs for sabotaging the Red Wolf Program just to protect her real estate deal.

"So they say." Al continues pacing, scratching the back of his neck. "Never believe the media. They lie about anything."

I attempt a gentler approach, though it makes me sick to pretend to care. "You loved her?"

He stares at me as if surprised I asked. "She was all I had."

"I'm sorry," I say as a feeling of disgust courses through my veins. This guy doesn't deserve any sympathy from anyone, especially me. "I know how you feel. You killed my Dad."

Al stops in his tracks. "No, you killed him. That bullet was meant for you."

The familiar feeling of guilt resurrects in my chest. I'm glad he doesn't check out my face, because I'm pretty sure I look like I'm going to cry. Which would only feed his crazy control issues even more.

He shrugs and paces again. Up and down the tiny passageways. "Good riddance anyway. He would have surely turned us in."

Anger boils beneath the surface but I mask it with a nod. "You're right. Listen, why don't you let me go and we'll call this thing even?"

Al chuckles. "I ain't as dumb as you think."

I want to say, *are you as dumb as you look?* But I refrain. No reason to fuel his fire. Right now, I need to butter this guy up until either I can get away, or until Mo can find a way inside.

I keep stalling. "How'd you find me? After all this time?"

He scratches the stubble on his face. "You were dumb enough to show your face on T.V. Lucky for me, I was watching that day. Saw the sign of this place and drove straight down. I figured I'd find you somehow. Had no idea you'd walk right into my open arms."

Mo mentioned the protest too. That thing brought Mo down, but it also brought Al. Dumb, dumb, dumb. I could kick myself for getting involved that day. I should have stayed hiding behind that truck. It's caused me nothing but trouble ever since.

And it may have cost Sadie and Dylan their lives.

I try to keep my voice soft and even. "So, what are you going to do now? If you let me go, maybe you can sneak out of here. Get away again."

"Yeah, you'd like that huh? You want to know what I'm going to do?" Al walks over to and gets in my face. The smell of beer clings to his breath.

"First I'm going to kill you—the way you all killed my sister. Then I'm going to find a way out of here and walk out scot-free. I just need to wait for a few things to fall into place."

The whole plan muddles in my brain.

My mind got stuck on the *kill you* part.

If captured, knowing the right moment to escape can be a critical part of getting away.

A voice from outside the house interrupts our little chat. "Al Smith. The place is surrounded. Let the hostage go and come out with your hands where we can see them."

My body relaxes. Sweeney's here.

My confidence boosts. Even I know that Al is out of Mo's league. Mo is strong and smart in survival. But Al is a whole different breed. Like a lion against a kitten. Al doesn't care who gets hurt and he's desperate. Not a good combination. Whereas, all Mo cares about is me being safe. Which makes him vulnerable.

Sweeney speaks into a bullhorn. "Come out with your hands up and we won't use force. Leave your weapon and the hostage inside until we have you in custody."

Al laughs and takes a swig of beer. He sneaks over to the window and peeks out. "These guys have their heads up each other's ass if they think it's going to be that easy."

He yells a few obscenities at the window. Not sure if they can hear him or not but it seems to make him happy.

Al twirls his knife and faces me. "Time to play."

My heart jumps. To be honest, I don't know why Al's even

keeping me alive. Unless he thinks it's safer for him to have me as leverage. Or unless he has other plans for me. I know one thing. I'm not going down without a fight. A lot has gone down in the last year and I've made it this far.

I've lost so much already that I have nothing else to lose.

I scoot to the edge of the couch and plant both feet on the ground. If this guy comes at me, I'm going to attack him with every ounce of fight I have. I keep my eyes on the knife in his hand. Knife fights are harder to control than gun fights. They usually end up with more wounds because it's up close and personal. Whereas with a gun, you have a better chance of getting away. However, the survival rate is better with a knife so in this case I guess you could say—in some sick way— that I am lucky.

Al will probably stab me, but my chances of living are better this time over last time.

Al moves toward me and stops a few feet away. He puts his knife in his belt and grabs a roll of duct tape out of his bag. "Forgive me for not trusting you."

He pounces like a cat on a molehill.

I scream as he yanks me to the floor. When he presses one knee in my chest, the breath is forced out of my lungs. I gasp for air as he duct tapes my hands together in front of me. Once he's done, he shoves a green bandana into my mouth. "For old time's sake."

I gag on the soiled cloth. Takes me back to the time when Al, and his buddy Billy, trapped me in the woods after finding me spying.

Only that time, Mo saved me.

This time, I'm on my own.

I flail around on the floor as he laughs above me, watching. Eventually, I give up and go limp from exhaustion. The cloth minimizes the amount of air I can suck in to catch my breath.

Al leans over me as I curl into a ball on my side. "I'm going to give your boyfriend a little love. Be right back." He peeks out the back door and then moves the furniture barricade aside. He cracks the door and sneaks out.

Meanwhile, Mo and Sweeney are in the front with who knows how many cops.

I try to scream for help but my voice is muffled. My arms are throbbing in pain from being yanked like they are going to rip from their sockets any minute now. I thrash around and grit my teeth as the pain gets worse.

Eventually I give up and lie on the stinky rug, watching the back door. Praying Mo will come busting through. Hoping to see Sweeney's face.

I hear noises outside. Clanging and twanging. But I can't make out what is going on.

My body has a delayed reaction to the adrenaline pouring through me. I start to hyperventilate. My lungs hurt from trying to take in huge gulps of air. My head is dizzy from the lack of oxygen. I use my tongue to try and move the bandana to once side, hoping to allow in a little air. I close my eyes and settle down. I can't freak out. That's exactly what Al gets off on. Panic and control.

I hear a couple gunshots and some yelling.

I wait, not knowing what to do.

Please let Mo be okay. The last time I lost him, I was lucky to get him back.

I can only hope my luck hasn't run out.

Pounding footsteps thump across the back of the house. A scream. Then a yell. Then another gunshot.

I stare at the door, waiting for the outcome.

Will it be the hero coming to rescue me? Or the returning villain?

The door bursts open and Al slides in, laughing. He slams

the door and races to the front window, peering through the sheets.

"Special delivery!" he yells out the glass.

Outside a horrible sound circles the building. Snarling, screeching, growling.

Al laughs with his back toward me. "Always did love a good show."

I try to work the bandana out of my mouth.

Al hears me struggling and pulls it out. "Wanna see for yourself?" He picks me up by my bound arms. Then he yanks me to the window and holds me against it.

Outside, the skinny lion charges the gate.

Before the group of men can barricade him, the lion bursts through and attacks one of the officers. Even though the animal is skinny and barely alive, he is also starving.

Sweeney draws his gun and fires.

I scream out as the poor lion crumbles to the ground.

I slide down the wall and hang my head.

"Awww, your people don't like them animals after all."

I don't take the bait he's dangling in front of me. Trying to egg me on. I need to keep pretending I'm on this lunatic's side until I can get away. "I guess not."

Al laughs from behind as the walls close in on me. He's obviously amused at the aftermath of his plan. "One man dead, one less animal in the world. I am 2 - 0."

"Can you please release my arms for a second?"

"Why should I?" Al looks at me sideways like a dog listening to a high-pitched sound. He removes his knife and pokes it into my cheek. "You gonna cause me trouble?"

"So I can get eaten by rabid animals or shot by those people? No thanks, I'm safer in here."

His eyes show a vulgar hunger and he licks his lips. "I can do more for yah. That's for sure."

Then his ears prick like a predator on the Serengeti. He

presses his back against the boxes and slithers around the room until he reaches the back door.

Meanwhile I sit on the floor and start working my hands out of the tape. Twisting and pulling. If I can get free and out that front door, I have a slim chance of surviving. Only I'm not sure how many lives I have left.

I stretch and rip and pull, keeping my eyes on Al in case he checks on me.

"I know someone's out there." Al mumbles through the curtain.

The tape loosens and I stop to make sure he didn't notice.

"Probably in the cages."

He places both hands on the glass and squints.

I move to my knees and wait. I judge the distance to the front door and then watch Al. He's so focused on finding a possible intruder, he doesn't realize I'm about to escape.

I breathe as I rise up to my feet, keeping myself calm, steady, and focused.

On the count of three in my head, I jump up and race to the front door, tripping over boxes and paper and junk.

I scramble for the door.

"Hey! Al hollers and charges after me.

I grab the top of a pile and pull it crashing down between us. Al barrels through the paper barrier like a bulldozer. My hand trembles as I fiddle with the chain lock, sliding it out of its groove. As Al fights his way over the pile of stuff, I throw open the door and run. "Help!"

The men still fighting off wild animals spin around.

But Mo and Sweeney are nowhere in sight.

Al grabs my hair and yanks me back inside when the back door explodes open.

"Freeze!" Sweeney yells. He holds up a gun and points it straight at us "You're done Al. Don't even try it."

Al's muscles tense as he grips me tighter. The knife comes

up to my throat again. "I'll kill her. I swear to God. Call your men back."

"Let her go, Al." Mo says calmly. He's standing right behind Sweeney.

Static comes across the radio and a group of men back up and step away from the lot of parked cars.

Al pushes me out the door. "Move it. No funny business."

I take small steps as he pushes me across the porch and down the stairs. Sweeney and Mo follow behind us. I can see them in my peripheral vision.

Al hollers commands. "Have them drop all the weapons. You too!" I hear a clank on the porch as a weapon falls from Sweeny's hands.

"Kick your gun to me." Al demands.

The gun slides across the planks.

"Pick it up." Al pushes me down to a kneeling position. I hand the gun to him. He puts the knife away and points the gun at my head.

I close my eyes and try to go somewhere else. The feeling of cold steel on your temple is enough to shut you down.

"Now, I'm leaving." Al pushes me toward the cars. He glances between the men at the fence and Sweeney and Mo who are still flanking us. "And I'm taking her with me."

"No you're not," Mo says. "I won't let you."

I want to keep my eyes on him, but I don't want to see fear in his eyes. Or hopelessness. I know—as well as he does — that if Al gets me in that car, I don't have much hope of getting out of here alive.

A squeaky sound draws my attention away from morbid thoughts of a sure death.

The skinny mommy monkey peeks around the side of the house. She squeaks again and then scans the yard nervously. When she spots me, she whimpers and lumbers toward me, carrying her dead baby in one arm. I want to make a loud noise, maybe shoo her away, but Al prevents me from making any movements.

She stops every few feet to assess the danger level. Each time, she moves closer and closer.

Al obviously hasn't seen her yet. Maybe he doesn't care. Maybe he's watching Mo and Sweeney. Or maybe he's preoccupied with getting to the car alive.

The mommy monkey races in my direction. When she reaches me, she clutches my ankle and squeaks again.

I shake her off with the hopes of scaring her away.

"What the hell...?" Al kicks the monkey. She tumbles across the yard, dropping her dead baby on the soft grass. But she quickly gets back up, picks up her baby, and comes toward me again. This time, she is more cautious. And this time, her hand stretches out as if asking for food.

I don't want Al to kick her again. She can't handle that many harsh blows. This time, I gently nudge her away with my toe. She pauses and stares with round eyes. She doesn't understand why I'm pushing her away. I nudge her again, this time a little stronger.

Please, please go away before you get hurt.

"I'll take care of this." Al raises his gun. "Bye bye, little monkey."

I yell at him, "No! Don't!"

He fires and the bullet hits the monkey in the leg.

I scream as she drops to the ground. She crawls across the grass with her foot dragging.

Al raises his gun again. Even as hurt as she is, she crawls straight to her dead baby. She's still protecting something that is gone. Because that's what she's supposed to do. Tears well in my eyes.

"So long, monkey." Al says.

Rage burns inside me.

When he lifts the gun, I swing around and grab his wrist.

We struggle with the weapon until he punches me a couple of times in the ribs. But no matter what he does, I refuse to let go. We fight and twirl around, but I tire faster. He's twice as heavy and his grip three times as strong. He pries the gun from my hand and points it in my face.

A heavy load slams into Al, knocking us both off our feet.

My head hits the ground and I see nothing but a yellow blur pouncing out of the woods.

Even if you are rescued, the fear can follow you if you let it.

Cat attacks Al.

They wrestle along the ground. She snaps her teeth a few inches away his face. The shrieking sounds that come from her are primal and send chills scaling my spine.

She's defending me.

My ears buzz and for a second the world flips on mute. I try to stand, but the blow has knocked my equilibrium off center. The ringing in my ears throws off my balance.

Suddenly, Mo is at my side. He pulls me to my feet but my legs won't hold my weight. I stumble and fall to the ground.

He tries to lift me and lead me away from Cat, who's clawing at Al's back, snapping and snarling. Mo's mouth moves, but I can't make out what he's saying. My ears are buzzing. Ringing.

I push his hand away and crawl to the mother monkey. She's lying on her side, covered in blood and licking her foot.

At first, when she's sees me, she cowers. Like an abused puppy.

"It's okay."

When she hears my voice, she slowly slinks toward me, dragging her foot behind her.

I hold out my hand and wait. She puts her tiny little fingers in my palm. I pick her up and hold her close to my body.

"Grace?" Mo's voice sounds muffled, but at least I can hear him.

"Yeah?"

He touches my shoulder softly. "Are you okay?"

I try to keep the tears hidden and shake my head. "No."

"Let me." He holds out his shirt. When I place the wounded monkey in his hands, he swaddles her up in the cloth. "Let's go."

A yelp catches my attention. I wobble on my feet and look over my shoulder.

Al throws Cat off his back and kicks her in the side. She hisses and crouches on the ground, obviously hurt. Al grabs his gun. He raises the weapon again.

Cat paces back and forth, growling and snarling. She has no clue about the dangers of a gun.

I half run, half hop. At the last minute, I throw myself in front of Cat just as the weapon explodes.

The bullet rips through my thigh.

Al tries to fire again but his gun jams. "Damn!" He hits the gun against his side.

I crumple to the ground and writhe in pain. Blood pours from my leg.

Mo slides in next to me, still holding the monkey. "Jesus, Grace. What did you do that for?"

"I had to."

Mo presses his free hand on my leg. Blood pumps through his fingers. He appears worried and checks the hole. "You're okay."

"Liar."

Cat is back on her feet and stands in front of Mo and me.

Al points his gun at us. "Isn't this sweet?"

Luckily, Sweeney fires first. A burst of blood comes out of Al's side. He drops the gun and grabs his leaking stomach.

Sweeney jumps him and pins him to the ground. Another officer races over and holds down Al's legs.

Al thrashes under two men. "Get off me!"

"You are under arrest, Al Smith." Sweeney waits for the officer to cuff Al. "For everything."

Al's face is already pale as a ghost as the life slowly drains out of him. "Get me a lawyer."

Sweeney drags him to his feet and arrests him. "You have the right to shut the hell up."

The last words I hear out of Al's mouth when they drag him past me are, "Bite me."

The men fight him and drag him by both arms to a squad car. A blood trail marks his path. Before Sweeney forces him in the car, Al turns and stares. A smiles draws across his face as he puckers his lips in a kiss.

The look chills me to the bone.

Al might be leaving, but he'll never be gone from my life. No matter how much I try to forget him. His actions and his face have scarred my heart.

I don't move until the car drives away.

A long breath seeps out. I'm finally safe.

Mo yells over me. "Medic! We need some help here now." He stays next to me and holds my hand. The monkey clings to his shirt, still wrapped in the cloth. "Hang in with me, Grace."

The exhaustion and pain hit me. The dizziness makes me lay my head back on the ground.

Cat walks over and lies down next to me. She leans her head on my chest.

"Grace, how are you?" Sweeney asks.

"Couldn't be better."

He smiles and nods. "I need to take the panther. Have her checked out."

I stroke Cat's head as Sweeney circles a rope around her neck. He leads her away, followed by a USF officer who takes the monkey away from Mo.

I watch them place the animals in a truck and drive away. I scan the yard.

The dead bodies of zoo animals scatter the ground. The lion and a few I didn't expect: two wolves, a Grizzly bear, and a few hyenas.

I couldn't protect them all, but at least I saved a couple. Cat and the monkey survive.

Birdee's voice floats down the hill. "Grace!" When she spots me, she shoves her way past an officer who tries to block her.

Seconds later, she hobbles down the hill with her hands on her hips. She stops when she reaches me and frowns. "Grace Wells, you're killing me. My heart can't take another heart attack. I'm an old woman, you know. Not as young as I look."

"Sorry, Birdee."

"Sorry, my butt. Jesus child, you're as white as an albino." Worry crosses her face and then she notices my thigh. She places one hand on the ground and kneels, landing gently on her bad knee. Her frown drops and her lips quivers. "Dear God. I'm sorry…"

"She's okay, Miss Birdee." Mo tries to reassure her. "I promise. An ambulance is on its way."

"Ambulance? My dead mother drives faster than them. Better off driving her yourself." She stares at Mo until he gets the hint.

"Oh, right!" Mo smiles and stands. "Let me see what I can do. Watch her."

She pulls me into her. "Thank God, you're okay, Chicken. I don't know what I would do without you."

"Ditto." I squeeze her hand and search the line of people gathering on the road, "Where's Mom?"

She pats my head and pulls back, still assessing my condition. "When Sweeney told me you were shot, I came."

"Really?" Can't imagine why Mom wouldn't come down to see me—after all this. She'd never stay away unless.... unless something happened. Something's off.

I search Birdee's eyes for a reason. "What happened?"

She drops her façade, letting her shoulders sag forward. "Rex found Sadie."

"Thank God." A weight rolls off my shoulders as she explains.

She holds up her hand to stop me from saying more. "She's alive but she needs serious medical attention. May lose part of her leg."

"Oh." Though it doesn't surprise me. The bite was bad, and I'm sure it got worse out there.

"Rex drove her straight to the hospital. Sadie's mom was a complete and total wreck—as you can imagine— and she needed a ride to the hospital. Sweeney convinced your mom you were okay and headed to the same hospital. Your mom offered to drive Cammie and is waiting for you there."

It was especially hard on Mom the last time I was hurt. I'll never forget the expression on her face when she showed up at the camp and saw me alive. A look of anger mixed with relief mixed with sadness. She knows exactly how Sadie's mom feels, and that is why she went there with her. For support.

I'm almost afraid to ask my next question. "And Dylan? Did they find him?" His name hangs in the air. I linger in the space between hope and reality. I convince myself of the best outcome. Her answer could fall either way—found or lost; here or gone; alive or dead.

I hang my head, avoiding Birdee's eyes.

Though, something inside me knows Birdee's omission of Dylan's status isn't a good sign. I wait for the answer but no words tumble from Birdee's mouth.

When I glance up, she slowly shakes her head.

"Oh no." I hold my head in my hands and think of Dylan. How he charged off deeper into the swamp water to distract those men. To save Sadie. To protect me. I knew when we found his necklace he was probably gone, but I guess I hoped he'd somehow pull through. Beat the odds. Never expected someone as strong or as tough as Dylan to die.

Goes to show, you just never know.

"Poor Dylan." The words feel brittle on my tongue. "Rex okay?"

Birdee lets out a long sigh and adjusts her hat. Her eyes water and glisten a bright blue. "I hope so. He's the one who found Dylan's body."

To think of Rex, out searching in the Everglades for his nephew, breaks my heart. I know what it's like to think someone is alive, only to lose them in the end.

We both hug for a few seconds until Birdee whispers in my ear, "Grace."

"Yeah?" I whisper back.

"Don't move." She hisses.

"Why?"

Her warm breath heats my ear. "There's a huge animal staring right at me."

I slowly turn my head. And come face to face with Hercules.

In the wilderness, you may have to do things you normally would not to stay alive.

The huge animal stands still like a statue.

Luckily there is some distance between us, at least fifty feet. From this distance, I can't see the expression on his face. Don't know whether he's mad, hungry, or confused at all the visitors lingering around his home.

Like he knows nothing here will ever be the same again.

I can relate.

He shifts his beady eyes from Birdee and me. He crouches and picks up one paw and steps forward.

"Get up slowly." Even though my leg is on fire with pain, I force myself to stand, keeping Birdee behind me. She must be scared because she doesn't object. And that happens...never. "Walk back slowly."

Birdee and I take a step back.

Hercules bares his fangs and roars.

Mo calls out softly from behind. "Grace, your knife."

"Hercules, it's okay." I reach down and grab the handle. I don't want to use this so I try to talk to the cat. This seems stupid but I try anyway. Maybe somewhere inside, he will recognize his name and stop stalking us.

We retreat another step.

Hercules advances. His lips are bared, showing his long fangs.

I hiss over my shoulder. "Birdee, I want you to get to the fence and climb over."

"The hell I am," she barks, causing the animal's ears to twitch. She lowers her voice but I hear the tremble in her voice. "I'm not leaving you."

"Go. Now." My voice cuts off each word from connecting to the other. When she doesn't budge, I push her hand off my shoulder without turning around. "Now...or we'll both die. Just trust me."

Birdee stands firm for a second and then submits to my demands. I hear her reversing.

The animal looks past me, watching her move.

"Walk slowly."

"Only way I can move, child."

I hear Mo's voice behind me, "Few more steps Birdee and you'll be at the fence."

Seconds later, I hear the chain link clang as someone grabs it.

The cat snaps his head high and stops swishing his tail. On high alert. Still eyeing Birdee as his new prey.

I move to the left a few steps away from Birdee and wave my arms, gripping my knife in one hand. "Hey! Over here!"

Mo speaks through gritted teeth. "What the bloody hell are you doing?"

"Distracting him."

Hercules glances at me. Birdee tries to climb the fence, but her foot slides out from under her and she falls.

This is all Hercules needs.

I take a few more steps into the middle of the yard and yell louder. "Hercules! Over here!"

Instead, the liger charges forward. His leg muscles ripple

and his ears flatten against his skull. This gorgeous hybrid is the perfect killing machine. Strong and fast with sharp senses. How in the world did Bob think he could control such a beautiful, yet massive creature like this?

"Hey!" I scream. Hercules slows for a split second.

This time, he forgets about Birdee, who's just cleared the fence, and sprints toward me. He makes a series of grunts and growls that send chills rippling down my spine. Sounds like one of those big Harley motorcycles trying to start up.

When Hercules gets too close, I turn and bolt toward Mo—limping from my bullet wound leg.

"Run!"

I glance over my shoulder. Hercules gains on me. Fast.

At the last second, I stop and turn, catching the liger off guard.

When he skids up close, I swing the knife from left to right in a wide arc. The sharp blade nicks his shoulder. A switch flips as he changes from a crazed lion into a wounded kitty. He snorts a few times and backs up, confused that his meal fought back.

This is my chance.

I race toward Mo, still standing by the fence. "He's coming. Run!"

Birdee yells from the safe side, "Someone shoot it! Now!"

I hear the lumbering of Hercules' huge padded paws as he shakes the earth with his weight. Just when I reach the fence, he slams into my back. The knife pops out of my hand and I fall to the ground. I quickly cover my neck with both hands and curl in a ball.

"Hey!" Mo slams a large stick across Hercules' back.

The liger turns and growls, ready to fight.

I spot Al's gun a few feet away, still lying on the ground in the weeds. I crawl over to it and grab it. When I flip on my back, the liger attacks Mo. Screams and snarls blend together.

I close my eyes and fire.

The noises stop and everything goes quiet.

Except for the nagging voice in my head reminding me that I've killed a beautiful animal.

I open my eyes and see the huge liger lying on its side. I hobble over to Hercules, still holding the gun in case he jumps up and attacks as a last ditch effort.

Chest wound. He doesn't stand a chance. He's breathing but his eyes are closed. Without any concern for myself, I drop down next to him and press my hands over the gunshot wound. Blood pumps through my fingers at an alarming rate, but Hercules is still alive.

"Can someone help me?"

None of this was Hercules' fault. Being bred and raised by an idiot animal abuser was not his choice. Being born was not his choice. Dying is not his choice either.

It was mine.

But none of this had to happen.

This is why I try so hard to protect every animal. They don't have a choice like we do. To be good or bad. To be hungry or fed. Animals are just what they're supposed to be. They know it and they own it.

They don't worry or hold grudges or stress about life. They certainly aren't afraid of dying. It's part of their everyday world.

Which has somehow also become part of mine this last year.

In his last few moments, I wonder if Hercules knows what's happening. Knows he's going to die. He inhales one large breath and then sighs long and hard. A release. Then his eyes roll in his head and his large body sags into the earth.

I put two fingers on his neck, searching for a pulse, but he's gone.

I hang my head and cry. Nothing but death surrounds me. Animals and humans. Friends and foes. And as each day passes, I'm not sure why I'm here in this world if I can't make a difference with anything. Anywhere.

Mo and Birdee walk up.

"It's not your fault, Chicken." Birdee strokes my hair.

"She's right." Mo kneels beside me and kisses my forehead. "This cat would have killed you in a heartbeat."

"I know," I mumble.

Neither says another word nor do they feed me any more crap or try to make me feel better. They know me. They know there's no way I could ever feel good about any of this.

I've killed two things in a few days. A human and an animal.

Who's to say which life was worth more?

And while both deaths bother me, for some strange reason, killing Hercules hurts the worst.

They let me cry for a few minutes until I wipe my face and pull it together. The only thing I'm thankful for is that Birdee and Mo are alive.

"Come on. Let's get you to the hospital."

I glance back at Cat and the monkey in the back of the van. "What about them?"

"Sweeney will take care of it."

Mo lifts me up in his arms and I rest my head on his shoulder. Tears cloud my vision and pain suffocates my thoughts. Mo carries me to the ambulance and they give me something. After that, I fade in and out between reality and La-La land. I know Birdee and Mo ride with me in the ambulance because I hear them talking. The siren is loud, but eventually it fades into the background too.

The medics wrap me in warm blankets, poking me and moving me.

I hear them calling out codes and numbers.

But I'm not sure what anyone says or what anything means.

I finally let myself shut down.

SURVIVAL SKILL #27

Once you are rescued, the recovery process—mentally and physically—can be hard.

At the hospital, I wake up with a nurse wheeling me out of one bright room and into another.

The minute I open my eyes, it's like I've morphed into someone else. I might appear to be the same on the outside, but on the inside, something very different has invaded my body. Dulled the real me.

A body snatcher.

Whatever medicine they gave me must have worked because I feel abso-bloody-lutely nothing. Too bad nothing stops my brain from processing.

My head fills with the deaths of Annie, Bob, Hercules, and Dylan, even Junior.

It's all I see. It's all I think about. Everything else—any remaining good—has slipped away.

When they move me to the bed and leave, Birdee's face comes into focus. She kisses my cheek. "Chicken, you okay?"

I nod, causing the world to crash around in my head. Throbbing and pulsing.

I wince as Mom's face appears over me. Like an angel.

She strokes my hair. Her eyes are swollen and red, telling

me she's been crying very hard and very long. She sucks in air as if to force back her raw emotions. "I love you, baby. Thank goodness you are okay."

Birdee holds up a box of Moon Pies.

"Birdee!" Mom says. "Did you sneak those in here?"

"Yes I did. Don't say I never brought you anything." She opens them and hands me one. She leans in and whispers, "And I think they're much better than that young man's flowers."

I glance over at the table and see a huge colorful bouquet of Gerber daisies.

I smile and try to sit up. "Never too wounded to eat these." I force my tongue to move but it feels fat and hairy in my mouth. Maybe from the drugs they're giving me.

"That's my girl." Birdee picks up the chart at the end of my bed. She uses the pen and scribbles something. "Says right here, just what the doctor ordered."

Mom snatches the chart from her. "This is illegal."

Birdee frowns. "So I get arrested. What's the charge? Moon Pie distribution."

Mom groans as Birdee laughs.

I can't help but giggle softly. Pain shots through my leg. "Stop. It hurts to laugh."

"You better hide those. Don't let this old lady get you in trouble." Mom pats my hand. "Mo's right outside. He's been waiting here all night, so let me tell him you're awake." She kisses my forehead and leaves.

Birdee hobbles after her. "I need to talk to that damn nurse. Can't they see you're bleeding? Your dressings need changin'."

I glance at my leg, wrapped in blood stained gauze. "I'm sure there are people in here worse off than me."

"Maybe," Birdee says. "But they aren't lucky enough to be my granddaughter. So, too damn bad for them." She holds the door handle and winks. "Don't tell your mom I cussed in a hospital or she'll have my hide. Cussing and smuggling in sweets is not really her thing." She heads into the hallway to terrorize some poor candy striper.

The door opens.

I turn my head and see Mo walk in.

And, my world is okay again.

He's wearing the same clothes but his face is scruffier and his hair is messier. He walks up to my bed. "You awake?" When I nod, he walks over. "Well Blossom, you definitely keep things exciting."

My mouth is dry so it's hard to talk. "Yeah, that's me. All danger and daring." I cough and pain rips through my thigh. "Ah...my whole body hurts."

He grabs the small stool and rolls it under his butt. I don't know why but a random thought scrolls across my brain, *that's one lucky stool.*

He pours a glass of water and holds it to my lips. When I'm done, he rests his chin on my chest like a little cat looking for love.

I look down over my nose. "Go ahead. I can tell you want to say something."

He grins. "You look smashing."

"Ha!" I stroke his messy hair. "That's not what you really want to say."

He shrugs innocently. "Oh. I love you?"

I shake my head, which feels like a bell gonging inside. "Noooo."

"Don't have the faintest idea of what you mean then." He sits up in the chair and presses his warm hand against my forehead. "Then again, maybe you're delirious."

"That...you were right. I was wrong." I lay my head back and wait for him to come clean.

"Blossom..." Mo leans over and lightly kisses the bandage

above my eye, like a butterfly whisked by and lightly brushed over my skin. "...I don't need to say that."

"Well I do."

He wrinkles his too perfect nose. "Yeah? Well you can criticize yourself for both of us then." This time he leans over me and drops a light kiss on my lips. "I'm glad you're tough, Grace Wells. My life would tank if you weren't here to keep it lively."

I grin like a stupid girl. "Ditto, Mr. Cameron."

He sits back in the chair and holds my hand between both of his. "You had a chance to see Sadie yet?"

And back to reality. "No. No one has said anything about her. Is she still here?"

"Down the hall."

"Will you take me to see her?" I push up to a full sitting position and force myself not to wince. If he sees me in pain then he probably won't let me even pee by myself. I've already used enough Free Humiliation cards with this guy.

"Sure you're up for it?"

Not in the slightest. But, I lie anyway. "Yes, of course."

He stands and helps me out of bed. This takes longer than I expect with the bruises to my limbs, a concussion to my head, and bullet wound to the leg. He supports my elbow as I hobble out to the hall. The world is not quite straight, slightly tilting to one side. But I stay focused.

Birdee gives me the thumbs up. "That's my girl."

Mom stands and rushes over. "You sure you're okay to walk? It's not too soon?"

I try hard not to show any pain on my face. "Mom, I have to see Sadie."

"Her father is in there now."

A tall handsome man, dressed in a fancy navy suit, steps out of Sadie's room, which is only a few doors down the hall.

Then minute he sees me, he beelines straight for me. A

few young men with cameras charge down the corridor after him.

I grip Mo's arm and brace myself.

As he gets closer, I notice he's frowning. My heart speeds up. "Is Sadie alright?"

"For now." He says then he narrows his eyes. "You're Grace Wells, aren't you?"

"Uh yeah...I mean, yes sir, I am." I hold out my free hand to shake his but he ignores my gesture and folds his arms across his chest. A few bodyguards flank him, keeping the media at bay as they yell questions over the mayor's shoulder.

"How is Sadie?"

"Do you think this will impact your position on the Everglades Conservation Project?"

"What does this say about roadside zoos in the state of Florida?"

He pretends not to hear them. A learned skill because my head is already pounding again. "How could you do this?"

At first I'm not sure I heard him correctly. "Excuse me?"

He glances back at the growing crowd and lowers his voice so the reporters can't hear. "Why did you leave my Sadie out in that forsaken swamp...alone?"

"I...I didn't."

"You didn't? What do you mean, you didn't?" He moves closer to me. "From what I gather, you're the one who dragged my baby girl into this mess anyway. Is that right?"

I draw my head down like a turtle. At first, I want to defend myself, but technically, he's right. If I hadn't gone looking for Cat at Bob's, Sadie and Dylan wouldn't have been grabbed that night. Bob would have just snatched me. Which means they would both be here now.

"Yes. I guess so."

"You *guess* so?" He snaps the words in half with his tone.

Mo squeezes my hand as my legs start to tremble from the weight. "Sir, this is not Grace's fault."

Sadie's dad bites his lip in anger, trying to keep himself composed. The crowd grows and more people yell questions, making the hall smothering and loud. The mayor grows more and more flustered. "Well it's someone's fault."

Birdee speaks up from behind. I didn't even know she was listening. "Sir, not to be rude, but if you want to blame someone, blame yourself for allowing those kinds of places to stay open in the first place. That's the true crime."

"Birdee..." I say.

She holds up her hand and walks between us, her head craning back so she can see his face. "No, it's true. That place was atrocious, and so was the horrible man running it. So if you want to blame someone, the only options I see are you or those men, some of which are probably still out there hurting other people as we speak. So instead of picking on a wounded girl who saved lives, I suggest you get to your office and get some men out in those swamps to find them. While you're at it, make some real laws that make sure none of this ever happens again."

The mayor appears flustered and has no response.

Leave it to Birdee to tell a politician off. Just like that.

A reporter breaks through the line and jams a mic in my face. "Grace Wells, what do you think about the mayor's policy on roadside zoos?"

The mayor brightens up and throws his arm around my shoulders, speaking louder than he has been this whole time, making sure everyone hears his speech. "Grace and I both agree that right now, our focus is on getting my Sadie better. Bringing these men to justice. All the other stuff can wait. Right, Miss Wells?"

"I agree we should bring these men to justice." Birdee gives me the don't-put-up-with-his-bullshit-look.

This is my time to stand up for something. By my choice. Not because it was forced on me.

I remove the mayor's draping hand. And attempted control. "But...no offense Mr. Mayor, but I think your policies on roadside zoos and conservation stink. So I'd like to see that addressed in your upcoming election."

That felt good. I can't help but smile inside.

As I hobble away, the mayor gets hit with a barrage of questions and reporters asking him to comment on my comment about his comment.

When I glance over my shoulder, the mayor locks in on me.

Although I've never met him before, I can already tell he doesn't like me.

Not one bit.

SURVIVAL SKILL #28

Stay strong. Sometimes even the strongest people have weak moments.

W hen my eyes fall on Sadie, I pause.

She appears tiny. Like she's withering. Wilting. Sinking. Or she's being swallowed by the hospital bed.

After sitting me in the chair by her bed, Mo kisses the top of my head and tells me he will wait right outside for me when I'm done.

Sadie's eyes are closed. I watch her breathe and remain quiet so as not to disturb her. She has scratches all over her face and bruises on her eyes. Her arm is in a cast, and who knows what's going on with her leg. Mo only mentioned the infection was bad and they didn't know yet if they were going to amputate.

Here's a girl I've known only for a few days, yet it's like I almost lost the friend of a lifetime.

Tears poke at my eyes and slide down my cheeks.

I'm too sore to even wipe them away so I let them flow.

I lightly touch Sadie's hand and rest my forehead on the side of the bed.

Poor Sadie. Heartbroken. Defeated. Damaged.

I can't help but wonder how she's feeling inside. Because I

know she loved Dylan the same way I love Mo. I remember how horrible and lost I felt when I thought Mo was dead. Empty. Alone. Even the brightest sun always came with a shadow that seemed to follow only me.

I am heartbroken for Sadie and everything she's lost. Or is about to lose.

"Jeez, I get a little lost and hurt my leg...suddenly everyone gets all emotional on me. But I didn't expect you to crack so easily." The voice is deep and raspy.

I lift my head and realize Sadie is the one talking.

I quickly wipe my face with both hands and sit up. "Sadie. Thank God you're alive." I lean over and gently hug her.

She pats my arm. "Ditto."

I smile faintly. "You okay?"

"I think so."

We both stare at each other for a few seconds. Like the world has stopped turning, allowing thoughts to sneak in. Neither of us says a word. What is there to say anyway? Every sentence that pops into my head seems stupid and shallow.

I swallow hard and eventually choose the only words I can manage. "I'm so sorry."

"Don't." Sadie shakes her head. "Don't do dare that. This isn't your fault. We all make our own choices. Me. You. Dylan. He made the wrong one...he never should have tried to save us. Stupid hero. Serves him right."

I sit quietly as her moods shifts from sadness to anger.

"I mean, what an idiot! What did he think he was doing anyway?"

I keep my voice low. "Saving us. Saving you. Seemed brave to me. At the time."

Yeah?" She shifts in her bed. "Well, you see where that got him? Freakin' *dead*!" She yells the last word and then stares out the window.

I bite my lip to keep from crying. This all brings back my feeling for Mo when I thought he was gone. He stayed back to fight those men off. To save Dad and me from Al. He got shot, and when I thought he was dead, all that was left was anger and sadness.

Only I got him back.

That won't happen here. Dylan's body has already been recovered and identified by Rex.

If Sadie doesn't want me to cry, I won't. If she wants me to get angry with her, I will.

"Jerk. Thought he was invincible." Then I hear her sniff but her head is turned away from me so I can't see her face. "Doesn't matter. He's gone and he wouldn't want us whining on about him."

"That's probably true," I whisper. All I can do is agree with what she says. No use arguing. No use giving her my opinion. She's the one who lost someone, so she can say and do whatever she wants. Who am I to go against her? I clutch her hand. "You going to be okay?"

A tear trails down the tip of her nose. "I'm alive, aren't I? So don't feel sorry for me."

"Okay."

"I mean, people die every day. Right?"

"True." I say softly.

She sucks in a breath. "It's life, right? You know. Everybody dies at some point."

I nod. "Doesn't make it easier."

"Definitely sucks." Sadie's face pinches in pain and her voice breaks when she speaks. "But...who's going to put up with my shit now?"

My throat burns from trying not to make a sound. From holding back my sobs. It's hard because not only did I adore Dylan, I feel horrible. Not to mention, I understand her pain. I've been where she is now. With Mo and Dad. I squeeze her hand. "I will, Sadie."

Her sharp eyes soften and glisten with tears. She puts her hand on top of mine and holds on as the dam breaks tears stream down her face. "What am I going to do?"

"Oh Sadie. I'm sorry."

She covers her face with her hands. "What am I going to do without my Dylan? Without my soul mate?"

I shake my head and a tear rolls down my face. It kills me to see her cry. It also brings back how much I miss my dad. It never gets easier; it just gets hidden, buried away. But it's always there, trying to surface. "I...I don't know."

She crumbles. "I loved him so much."

"I know." I stand even though my leg and side are killing me and crawl onto the bed next to her. I put my arm around her and pull her head onto my shoulder. She lets it all out, sobbing in my arms. Her shoulders shake and she gasps for air. I can't help but cry along with her.

There's nothing else I can do or say.

Dylan's dead and he's never coming back. Now, Sadie has to deal with life on her own.

Sadie and I sit together and cry. Mo peeks in the window a few times.

I shake my head, telling him not to come in. Not now. Sadie needs me.

Then he comes back and holds up my box of Moon Pies.

"Wait here. I'll be right back."

I limp to the door. Mo hands them to me through the crack. "Thought these might help. No cupcakes around."

I lean out and kiss him. "Thank you."

"For what?"

"For being you." I look back at Sadie, feeling a little guilty that I get to keep Mo when she lost Dylan. "I'm going to stay in here a while."

He nods and smiles, "Okay, but you better save me one."

I shuffle back to the bed in pain, but I hide it. No amount of pain amounts to what Sadie is going through now. "I have something that might cheer you up."

"That's impossible." Sadie sniffs, lying on her side, facing away from me.

"Trust me." I sit next to her and pull out the box of Moon Pies. "Ta da!"

Sadie smiles when she sees the box. "Are you serious?"

"My dad always told me Moon Pies can't make me feel good, but they can make me feel better."

Sadie wipes her swollen face with her nightgown sleeve. "Well I heard he was a pretty smart man. So, who am I to go against him?"

"That's what I'm sayin'." I open the box and hand her a chocolaty treat.

I unwrap one too.

She holds hers up. "To Dylan."

I clink my Moon Pie with hers. "To Dylan."

We both eat the delicious treat in silence. Fine with me. We don't need to talk. And I have nowhere to go. I plan on staying with Sadie as long as she needs me to.

For once, I finally have a friend.

A real friend.

A girl friend.

And I will help her through this.

Because I can.

One Moon Pie at a time.

EPILOGUE

Never give up. Sometimes in any survival situation, all hope is never lost.

I'm losing track of time.

Sometimes the days go by so slow and I think about Dylan all day.

Other times, they go by so fast and I find myself shocked that it's already been a month since the funeral. Thirty days since I lost a friend and Sadie lost a love. Four weeks since my world was once again turned upside down.

Knowing Al is finally behind bars where he belongs is comforting.

I'm finally safe.

Now, I can go wherever I want. And I never have to look over my shoulder again.

Even though he's put away, Mom still ended up selling the house and I don't blame her. Our life there is over.

Now we can begin a new one, here with Birdee.

Rex has had a tough time with Dylan's death. Feels guilty. His sister, Dylan's mom, is back in South Africa with no plans to ever visit the Everglades again. It's hard to return to the place where you lost everything.

Mo and I sit on the back deck and watch the tourists go

through the channel in their loud airboats. I take a sip of Birdee's homemade lemonade topped with a sprig of mint.

I watch Mo play with the straw in his mouth.

Lucky straw.

It's been so nice having him around. But it's also been hard not getting much alone time with him. Birdee practically follows us around the house, making sure we don't get too much private time together. Our make-out sessions are minimal, always being interrupted by an overprotective mom and a nosy grandma. But they are always awesome.

As we sit on the porch swing, a warm breeze floats by.

Mo pushes a tuft of hair out of my face. "You look beautiful today."

"Thank you," I say, smiling. He grins. "Why do I feel like you're buttering me up for something?"

"I can't tell my girlfriend, the one I love, how gorgeous she is?" He smiles but shifts slightly on the chair, enough for me to notice. I have memorized his movements and can pick them out a mile away.

My stomach drops. "Wait, are you leaving?"

"Not today." He takes a sip of his drink. I watch a drop cling to his lips. Exactly what I would do if given the chance.

"What does that mean?"

I watch the moisture slide down his glass and fall into his hand. I put my glass down, feeling sick. I don't like how awkward he appears. Not to mention, he won't meet my gaze. "Well, I'm sure Birdee doesn't want me crashing on her couch forever."

"Don't put this on Birdee. What's going on?" The last time this conversation came up, Al was hunting me down and Mo left me in the Everglades so I'd be safe.

"Nothing." Mo turns toward me and relaxes when he sees my face. "Blossom, don't worry. I didn't mean to scare you."

I swallow hard. I will not cry. "Come on Mo, I can tell something is going on."

Mo kisses my hand and tries to rock the swing again. "I talked to Sweeney. He found a nature reserve for the monkey and Cat."

"Good." I keep both feet planted so we don't move any more. "And? What else? Does he want you to go back to North Carolina?"

"Not exactly," Mo says. He pushes his hands through his hair. The nervous twitch.

Please don't let this be bad. Please don't take him away from me.

"And?" I push him harder. I need to know. "Why are you being so vague?"

"I told him that I'm done helping him. It's not what I want to do anymore. This is over now and I need to move on."

I sigh a little. Maybe this means Mo will stay right here. With me.

"I've decided to take an internship at the Florida Fish and Wildlife." Mo glances down at my hand and plays with my fingers. Like he's afraid to see my expression when he drops a bomb.

All the possibilities race through my head. What could he possibly be doing that is so bad? "Thought you were already doing that? With Sweeney?"

"Yes, but I need to get away from this whole case." Mo says. "Find something different."

"I hope I'm not included in all that."

"No!" Mo practically shouts it in my ear. Then he drops his voice back to normal and smirks. "I mean no. I'm talking about Al. I paid a debt to my dad. And yours. But it's time to do something different. Something just for me."

The word hits my gut. I wish he had said 'us'. Do something for 'us'. 'Me' is singular. "Oh. So when do you leave then?"

"Not for a couple weeks. I wanted to spend more time with you."

Nausea ebbs and flows deep down. If Mo moves away then that means we won't see each other much. Maybe a weekend here and there, but how long does that last? I throw out my fear. "What about us?"

"Well...what about it?"

That hurt. I can practically see the imaginary dagger sticking out of my heart as it deflates. "Oh." That's all I can say. Tears threaten to reveal my fake composure. I look out at the airboats humming by so he doesn't see I'm upset. I'm sure it's written in big letters all over my face. I'm not good at hiding things. Especially my feelings.

Mo jumps off and squats in front of me to grab my attention. "Blossom...don't worry. I'm not giving up on you. Or us. That's why I've accepted the job in Miami. We'll be closer than ever."

"Wait, Miami?" At first, the word doesn't register. Then I realize what he means. I smile. "Oh! Miami?"

"It's the closest office I could find. Only one hour away."

I wrinkle my nose. An hour is still too long as far as I'm concerned but it's better than nine or ten.

"I can come see you every weekend once school starts." I groan. "You know, I have one more year."

Mo reaches behind him and pulls out a brochure. "Or...maybe you could do an internship."

I snatch the brochure and study it. "The Marine Mammal Center?"

He grabs it back and flips to a certain page. "Here. Look. It's perfect."

I read the internship section. Working with whales. Studying dolphins. My heart skips. "Oh my God."

Mo's smile sags. "What? You don't like it?"

I jump up and accidentally knee him in the chin. "Oi!"

I fall onto his lap and hug him, kissing his cheeks, eyes and nose.

He talks between kisses that I peck on each part of his face. "So you like the idea?"

"Abso-bloody-lutely! This is awesome. I can't believe it. Maybe Sadie can come with me. Of course I have to ask Mom first and make sure it's okay with my school. But I bet I could get ahead in fall and come down for the work program in the spring."

"I'll wait for you," Mo says. "Forever if I have to."

"Ah, I'm so relieved! I thought you were going to break up with me or something."

He appears hurt. "Grace Wells, I love you. Why in the world would you think that?"

I shrug. "I love you too. I thought maybe you...."

Mo cups my face and pulls me closer. He kisses me on the lips. Our mouths touch and struggle passionately as we smother each other with our breath. I can taste the lemon and lick a piece of sugar off his bottom lip.

"You think too much." He taps the tip of my nose. "I love you and want you to come with me. I don't ever want to be away from you again. Got it?"

I can barely breathe, lost in his eyes. "Sounds perfect to me."

As we sit staring at each other, taking each other in, Mo lightly traces my lips with his finger like he's painting a masterpiece. Every place he touches electrifies.

I love this guy and want so much to be with him. Like I've never been with anyone before.

The thought of moving to Miami. Working at a Marine facility. Doing what I love. And being close to the guy I love more than life is so exciting, I almost want to burst inside. Implode.

Finally, things are looking up.

Finally, I can live my life without being in fear.

Finally, love wins in the end.

And today, for the first time in a long time, I feel unstoppable.

THE END

ALSO BY SHELLI R. JOHANNES

Nature of Grace Series

YA Thrillers

Untraceable

Uncontrollable

Unstoppable

Loves Science Series

The Loves Science books introduce readers to basic concepts of science, technology, engineering, and math, and are perfect for the classroom.This STEM series is perfect for fans of *Ada Twist, Scientist*, and anyone who enjoys asking questions.

.

Theo TheSaurus series

Theo TheSaurus is a little dino who loves words--the bigger the better!

"A well-armored sesquipedal-o-saur picks a "quintessential" companion in his second outing. The theme of finding and sharing a common language adds a buff to the basic vocabulary building. Dinophiles and budding wordsmiths will be delighted."- Kirkus Reviews

.

Standalones

Shine Like a Unicorn (picture book)

Penny The Engineering Tail of the Fourth Little Pig (picture book)

Florence Nightingale (She Persisted series chapter book)

Dear Reader,

When I started this series, I had no idea if it would ever see the light of day. I needed to continue publishing books in the Nature of Grace series with the hope of making a difference in this world.

This time, *Unstoppable* spotlights the plight of the Florida panther as well as the problem of pop-up roadside zoos. The Florida Panthers once roamed freely, but are at the top of the long list of endangered animals.

The idea to take Grace to the Everglades was an easy one. I grew up in Vero Beach, Florida and we used to visit the Everglades and swamps when I was little. I remember the time my dad took my brother and me hiking in the swamps at dusk. We walked out on an old crickedy wooden bridge with nothing between us and the alligators. The thing that sticks out to me the most is seeing the glowing eyes in the water. I was terrified that day and am sure those alligators were hoping for an early dinner.

Unstoppable is my way of shedding a ray of light on a problem we don't know much about. The problem surrounding roadside zoos is alive and well. The limited and loose restrictions on purchasing wild or exotic animals is a real one.

With this book, I hope to create awareness around their story and struggles.

Just as in *Untraceable* and *Uncontrollable*, this book is still thrilling and mysterious with a strong girl character, two hot boys, and some great kissing. :) But in the end, my underlying purpose is to inform my readers of atrocities to animals and nature.

I hope you like reading *Unstoppable* as much as the first two. If you find yourself bothered or angry with some of the issues discussed/raised in this book, please see my "Call to Action" section so you can find your own way of making a difference, big or small.

I would love to hear from you anytime! I make an effort to respond to reader and blogger email timely. After all, you all are the reason I write! Feel free to email me at shelli@srjo hannes.com or visit me at my website srjohannes.com where you can sign up for my newsletter.

Best,
Shelli

CALL TO ACTION!

You can make a difference!

Here are some quick and easy actions you can take from your own home.

To find out more about the Florida Panthers in *Unstoppable***:**

1. Read about the endangered Florida panther.
2. Help save the Florida panther by donating to the conservation fund dedicated to their ongoing protection and survival.
3. Sign a petition to save the Florida panthers.
4. Adopt a Florida panther as a gift for someone special.

To find out more about the red wolves in *Uncontrollable***:**

1. Find out more about the Red Wolf Recovery Program.
2. Learn about the Red Wolf Re-establishment Program at Alligator River National Refuge.

3. To sign a petition to bring back the red wolves or to save them from extinction.
4. Learn about the timeline of the red wolf.

To help the black bears in *Untraceable*:

1. Find out how the game show host, Bob Barker, has been working to close the bear pits.
2. Help Peta in their work to close Cherokee bear pits.
3. Join organizations that are helping to stop the illegal trade and poaching of the black bear such as WSA.
4. Find out more from WWF about bear illegal trading and the bile trade in Asia.
5. Find out about some campaigns to stop illegal wildlife trade.

ABOUT THE AUTHOR

Shelli R. Johannes is the award-winning author of the Nature of Grace novels including *Untraceable, Uncontrollable,* and *Unstoppable.* Since leaving Corporate America, she has followed her passion for writing and conservation by working with The Dolphin Project, the Atlanta Zoo, and others. She currently lives in Atlanta with a bird, two doodles, her British husband, and her kids, who she hopes someday will change the world. She also writes children's books.

www.srjohannes.com
shelli@srjohannes.com

facebook.com/srjohannesauthor
twitter.com/srjohannes
instagram.com/srjohannes
pinterest.com/srjohannes

ACKNOWLEDGMENTS

It's been three years since *Untraceable* was published. And it's been an amazing ride. I especially love the fan letters from all the teens that love animals and want to participate in nature conservation in some way.

To all the teachers, librarians, and booksellers for supporting this important book, especially Julie Stokes at Dalton Middle School for her undying support and constant texts of encouragement and silly things that make me laugh.

To the Indelibles, for staying by my side no matter what path I take.

To the Zeugma Institute for the support, love, and other 'writerly sh$t'."

To all the organizations for helping me in my research over the course of three books.

To Kate Tilton and Ashley for helping me stay organized and filling in the gaps I leave lying around.

To all my friends and book club for their support and for always asking about my books.

To Vania, once again, for bringing Grace (and all my characters) to life with her gorgeous photos.

To Jennifer Jabaley, Kristin Tubb, and Courtney Stevens for the awesome writing retreats and never-ending giggles.

To my beta readers and copyeditors for catching mistakes I miss and helping me grow as a writer with every revision.

To Kimberly Derting for always believing in me and being there when I needed to brainstorm, vent, or celebrate.

To the Thrill Seekers Street Team for their fandom and over-the-top support for all my work.

To my wonderful agent. Lara Perkins at ABLA, who not only gives kick-a$$ edits and advice but she also truly believes in me and my work. She sees all of my ideas as opportunities and not obstacles. That is hard to find in this industry.

To my family for keeping me real and grounding me, no matter what happens.

To my Goldendoodles, Charley and Dusty, for loving me no matter what mood I am in, good or bad.

To Madelyn and Gray, for loving me unconditionally and teaching me about the important things life.

To my hubby Ali, for never doubting me and for always putting my writing at the top of his long list.

Most importantly, to all my awesome readers/fans/bloggers, thank you for your undying support and for reading my books, especially out of the millions to choose from.